Ben Fine is a mathematician and professor at Fairfield University in Connecticut in the United States. He is a graduate of the MFA program at Fairfield University and is the author of fifteen books (twelve in mathematics, one on chess, one a political thriller and one a swashbuckler about pirates) as well over 130 research articles, fifteen short stories and a novella about pirates. His story *August 18, 1969,* published in the Green Silk Journal, was nominated for a Pushcart Prize. His story *From the Dambovitsa to Coney Island* was an honorable mention winner in the Glimmer Train Literary Contest. His story *The Schuyler Diamonds* won first place in the Writer's Digest Popular Fiction Awards in the Mystery/Crime Category. His story *My Mother, God, and the Big Blue Ford*, published in Green Silk Journal, won Honorable Mention in the 45th New Millennium Writing Awards. He has completed a memoir told in interwoven stories called *Tales from Brighton Beach: A Boy Grows in Brooklyn.* The stories detail his growing up in Brighton Beach, a seaside neighborhood on the southern tip of Brooklyn, during the 1950s and 1960s. Brighton Beach was unique and set apart from the rest of New York City, both in character and in time. His latest novel, *Out of Granada,* was released in 2017. His author website is https://benfineauthor.com

Ben Fine

THE THIN LINERS

AUSTIN MACAULEY PUBLISHERS™
LONDON • CAMBRIDGE • NEW YORK • SHARJAH

Copyright © Ben Fine 2024

All rights reserved. No part of this publication may be reproduced, distributed, or transmitted in any form or by any means, including photocopying, recording, or other electronic or mechanical methods, without the prior written permission of the publisher, except in the case of brief quotations embodied in critical reviews and certain other non-commercial uses permitted by copyright law. For permission requests, write to the publisher.

Any person who commits any unauthorized act in relation to this publication may be liable to criminal prosecution and civil claims for damages.

This is a work of fiction. Names, characters, businesses, places, events, locales, and incidents are either the products of the author's imagination or used in a fictitious manner. Any resemblance to actual persons, living or dead, or actual events is purely coincidental.

Ordering Information
Quantity sales: Special discounts are available on quantity purchases by corporations, associations, and others. For details, contact the publisher at the address below.

Publisher's Cataloging-in-Publication data
Fine, Ben
The Thin Liners

ISBN 9781643788630 (Paperback)
ISBN 9781643788623 (Hardback)
ISBN 9781645365426 (ePub e-book)

Library of Congress Control Number: 2024904882

www.austinmacauley.com/us

First Published 2024
Austin Macauley Publishers LLC
40 Wall Street, 33rd Floor, Suite 3302
New York, NY 10005
USA

mail-usa@austinmacauley.com
+1 (646) 5125767

One

I had gotten the address from the assistant director at High Ridge, found it pretty easily, and parked in front. The house was an older, beat-up Victorian on a quiet street in the north end of Stratford, near the Shelton line. It was built before 1920 and had a nice front porch, but it needed a paint job, a new roof and a lot of other work. It was the type of house that had probably been classy and perhaps fancy a hundred years ago when Stratford had some real life but like the town itself, it had gone to seed.

Paul Sojak owned the house and he had a license from the state to rent out rooms as a sober house. I phoned him from Danbury, told him my name and that I needed a room. He told me that he'd be at the place when I got to Stratford.

I climbed the front porch stairs, rang the bell and Sojak greeted me at the door. He was in his forties, medium build with dark hair, a scruffy face and he was wearing a deep-blue City of Stratford work shirt. Lucy, the assistant director who had given me the lead, told me that the Sojak house was registered at all the local rehabs. It was supposedly on the up and up.

"It will be one fifty a week and you have to pay in cash each Monday," Sojak told me as he showed me the room. It was tiny, with paint peeling off the walls and with a single bed, an old dresser and a worn-out mattress. "You can put in another dresser if you'd like, but not too much new stuff," he continued. "I got the place from my folks and I want to keep it up."

I looked at the cracked walls and the grime on what once were probably nice hardwood floors and said to myself, "Not doing such a good job keeping it up."

What could I do? I was living on the edge, and I needed a place. "I'll take it, Mr. Sojak," and I handed him the cash. He handed me an old, worn-out key that was greasy to the touch and I slipped it onto my key ring next to my car keys.

He smiled. "That's great, Cammond. Can I call you Don or Donnie? Call me Paulie. Everyone does. I drive a truck for the city and I'm in and out of the place. My girlfriend Mary and I have the big bedroom downstairs. Just so you know, there's two other renters. Eddie Maguire has the upstairs bedroom next to yours and Dan Scalise has the downstairs bedroom. You can use the kitchen. Make yourself a little spot for your food in the fridge and don't touch nobody else's."

We had walked through the kitchen to get to the room and it was a pigsty. There was an open bag of sugar on the counter which looked, even from a distance, like it was covered with a layer of grease, and a dirty coffee cup next to it. Connie, my ex-wife, would have had a hissy fit if she saw that. "There's going to be ants there, Donny," she'd probably screech in that tough voice of hers. She used to scrub our counters at least once a week and if I was going to put my food in that fridge, I'd have to clean it up a bit.

After he gave me the key, he handed me a sheet of paper that at first blush said all the right things. "Here are the rules, Cammond. You have to follow them." The sheet looked official, like it came from the state and listed what I could, and couldn't, do as a renter there. Although the sheet was clear, Paulie read the first three rules to me.

"Don, these are hard and fast regs. First; no drinking or drugs or I throw you right out the door."

I nodded. That one wasn't too hard. In my mind, I had won my battle with drugs and this was supposed to be a sober house. He continued.

"Second; there's a curfew at eleven in the evening unless you're working. Finally, no visitors alone in the rooms, so if you got a girlfriend, you got to take her elsewhere." I was alone with no prospects so these two were also easy.

Lucy at High Ridge warned me about Sojak. "Donny, be careful," she said. "It's a place to live and it's state-sanctioned, but I heard that Sojak is a grifter. Don't expect any help with your sobriety there."

She was right and it became clear to me quickly that the rules were bogus. All Paulie cared about was getting his cash each week.

Sojak left me alone, and I unpacked what little I had, and put some in the drawers and some in the small closet. Before the rehab I was living in a furnished room, so all my belongings pretty much fit into three big green garbage bags. What a come down from the tailored suits I used to get from Ferucci's. I carefully put the baby picture of little

Gene, my grandson, on top of the dresser. I've never seen him in person; my brother Mikey had gotten the photo for me. I then lay down on the bed. It was small and uncomfortable, but I still managed to fall asleep for a while.

Later that first night, I met Maguire, who had the room next to mine. He stumbled out of the bedroom to use the upstairs john and bumped into me. He was high as a kite – so much for not using in the Sojak house. Maguire was a thin fellow about forty-five and I tried to introduce myself.

"I'm Donnie Cammond. I just moved in." I held out my hand.

He grumbled, "Okay", ignored my hand and staggered by me. As my days in the Sojak house went on, I realized that he was a pill head who spent all day in his room sleeping. On my first Sunday living there, Maguire's wife and kids visited. She was a pleasant woman, plump in her mid-forties with two kids, a boy and a girl under ten. If I had wound up in a place like this when I was younger, I would never have let my kids visit. Maguire's family seemed to accept it and they all sat for a while and talked. His wife took his laundry with her. That night, late, I was in the kitchen and Maguire came in the back door holding onto a Spanish pretty boy in tight shorts and a black tee. They rushed by me and went upstairs and spent the rest of the night, and most of the next day, doing whatever they were doing in his room; so much for no overnight visitors.

The other renter, Dan Scalise, was a hefty bald retired firefighter about my age. He was hardly ever there and I didn't even meet him until the second week. Scalise told me that he was mandated to live in a sober house as part of a court order involving a DWI, but he spent most of his time at his girlfriend's. She came to pick him up when I first met him. I said hello to her but she was so drunk she could hardly answer me.

Sojak was a thin liner and I had him pegged right away. He was a grifter and a scammer, always looking for the quick buck. The bogus rules were one giveaway but what sealed it for me was when I noticed that all the household stuff; cleaners, paper towels, toilet tissue, even bar soap, was stolen from the city. In the driveway, Paulie had a collection of gas cans lined up. Each can had "City of Stratford" printed on the outside and he filled them for his own use whenever he filled the city truck that he drove.

"You need a job?" Paulie asked me that first day as I was carrying my stuff upstairs.

"No, I found something over at Rite-Aid on the Post Road. I start next week."

"Well, if it doesn't work out, and you need something, I got a friend who needs help. Just let me know."

There was no way; I told myself at the time, that I would get mixed up with a thin liner like Paulie. I should have listened to my own advice.

It wasn't easy for me moving in here. I rolled downhill for ten years and I knew I had hit rock bottom, but in my mind, I was still better than this. My folks would be rolling over in their graves if they could see where I was living. Quite a while ago I gave up thinking that I'd ever get my old life back, but it would have been nice to have a real apartment, a real job, some sense of stability and not living in a place like this with a bunch of thin liners.

My dad called them thin liners, so I always refer to them in the same way. They'd come into his paint store on Madison Avenue in the North End of Bridgeport and he'd watch them like a hawk. "Donny," he told me "they'll rob you blind. They're walking that thin line; honesty on one side and thievery on the other. You have to keep your eyes on them." If they tried some scam on him like, "Hey Mr. Cammond, I have a load of painting supplies at my house. I'll let you have them on the cheap," he always turned them down. "Donny," he lectured me when they left, "Don't ever start with them. Any paint they have was probably pinched from somewhere else."

One of the workers in the store, Joe Rattini, was a thin liner, constantly in trouble. My dad pulled me aside and told me about Rattini. "Donny, Joe's a hard worker but don't turn your back on him. Don't trust him further than you can throw him." Joe worked also as a night clerk at a motel on the Post Road and he got caught giving people rooms for cash.

Yeah, I've known these thin liners most of my life. They're not really hardened criminals. Oh, they'll steal; they'll rob you blind like my dad said. If they walk into a store and the cash register is open, and no one seems to be around, they'll gobble up the cash as fast as they can. But they'd never put on a ski mask and walk into a liquor store with a gun. No, their stealing is different; like Paulie, they're scammers; always looking for the easy buck, and for them, a few dollars scammed or pilfered is sweeter than the same few dollars earned. When my dad was young, there were probably more of them. Back then, a few bucks here and there could make a big difference.

Nowadays with things so expensive, for most people, the scamming isn't worth the effort, or more importantly, worth the downside.

Two

I'd been in the Sojak house three or four days when I finally met Mary Furillo, Paulie's girlfriend. My room had only one small window and had bad ventilation. It was too stuffy to sit in, so I began to sit in the small downstairs kitchen/dining room. Each day Paulie brought home a copy of the previous day's New York Times that he took from the library and I'd read it and do the crossword. Paulie had a collection of clocks on the dining room table that he claimed to be remodeling. I never saw him work on any, although he did move them around. I had to rearrange the clocks to make a place for myself.

I was working on the Times daily puzzle when Mary came out of their bedroom and into the kitchen. She was in her late twenties and not bad looking. She was wearing a tight-fitting blue dress that clung to her body and she was a bit heavy with dark hair, dark eyes, a big chest and nice legs.

"You're the new tenant, Donny, right?" She held out her hand to me.

I shook her hand and she smiled. "Want a cup of coffee?" she asked.

She seemed sweet and my first impression was that she was not so much a thin liner like her boyfriend but a lost soul.

She made us coffee and sat down across from me at the table. She moved one of Paulie's clocks and looked over at the puzzle I was doing.

"I try to read the New York Times, that's why Paulie brings it home," she started, "but it's hard. I always get lost in the articles. You must be smart. You're doing the crossword, I see. Those clues are killers."

She seemed really sincere and I did my best to be nice.

"Where are you from Donnie?" she asked me.

"I grew up on the North End of Bridgeport when it was still white. My dad owned a paint store on Madison Avenue. Nothing can't be fixed with a new coat of paint was one of his favorite sayings. We lived around the corner from the store." She was easy to talk to and I told her all this without thinking. I tend to talk too much but I try to play it close to the vest with people I don't know well.

She nodded and said, "Your dad seemed like he was a smart man also."

"He was okay," I told her "Came here from Scotland – spoke with a bit of a burr."

Her face showed no recognition when I told her that. "What's a burr?" she asked.

"You never heard a Scot speak? He'd roll his r's like Shrek." I then said ogre with my best cartoon imitation.

She laughed and stared at me with big doe eyes and then told me, "I grew up in Bridgeport also; down in Black Rock. My Dad has a stone business; he's a real greenhorn , can hardly speak English. My Mom works in the kitchen at Central High. The city gives insurance and they need the coverage."

"Really," I said. "I went to Central; played football there. I was an all-state linebacker but that was almost 40 years ago. My brothers played ball there also. My older brother Mikey had his house down in Black Rock. He was a Bridgeport cop but he's retired now and lives in Florida. It's a small world, eh Mary?"

She smiled and then we chatted a bit more and I finished the coffee. She then leaned into me and spoke a bit lower, almost secretively, "You're cool, Donny, but would you mind if I did a joint? If you're not cool with that because of sobriety or something, I'd understand."

"I don't mind – go ahead if you want." Weed never meant much to me either positive or negative.

She went into the bedroom and came out with a bone, lit it and took a hit. "I usually do one or two joints a day," she told me "It keeps me calm. At night sometimes I have some bourbon just to take the edge off."

As she smoked, I took a good look at her face. She was beginning to show the wasted look of a user; deep lines around her mouth and tightly drawn skin. She still looked young, but the young look was fading quickly. My Dad would have said, "Her face needs a good spackling." He looked at everything in terms of painting and remodeling.

Paulie and Mary were a strange couple, constantly fighting and then making up. He'd throw her out and then he'd ask her back. At one point, I came to the house and there was a Stratford work trailer parked in the driveway.

Paulie was in the kitchen so I asked him what the trailer was for.

"I'm going to have that stupid bitch live out there. Her parents won't take her back," he told me. The next day, though, the trailer was gone and Mary was back in the downstairs bedroom. Paulie alternated between treating her like a real lover and being totally a controlling asshole.

Thin liners aren't stupid, but they aren't clever either. They can never see more than one step ahead and simple scams always seem to go bad. After I knew him better, Paulie complained to me about some scam that he and his pal Goat had cooked up.

"Donnie, everything I try gets fucked up. If I had any luck at all. It would be bad luck. This had to work, Goat and I were certain and then they changed the fucking machine."

I wanted to shake him and tell him that his plans were stupid; there was no way in the world that they would work. But thin liners are dense and Paulie wouldn't have realized it even if I told him.

I liked Mary but she was dense also, not so much dishonest like Paulie but slow. She took classes at Housatonic Community College and she did all right in school, but most things were beyond her comprehension. She was in therapy, covered by her mother's insurance. The therapist had a nice office in an apartment building on Park Avenue in Bridgeport. One time she proudly told me, "Donny, you know after each session I give my therapist head. He loves it and he likes me so much, he gives me a fifty for it. It handles the weed for a few days. He's so cool, my therapist."

I wanted to tell her, "Mary, you're just hooking for him," but I didn't. She was clueless. To Mary, the therapist was kind to her, giving her the cash, and she was kind to the therapist giving him head. That was the only way she saw it.

Three

Lucille, the assistant director at High Ridge, who had given me Paulie's address, also gave me Ryan Foster's number for a possible job. Foster was the manager of a Rite-Aid Pharmacy on the Post Road in Stratford and was a recovering alcoholic himself who had been in rehab. Lucy told me that he took it upon himself to hire other recovering addicts that were referred to him. I gave him a call and met him at the pharmacy. He was a tall fellow, about my height or just a bit shorter, maybe six-one, slender with fair skin. He looked in his fifties and he must have been sober for quite a while because he didn't have the user look of a drinker or an addict. He led me into his office in the rear of the store and gave me an application to fill out. When I finished, he looked the papers over and then started to talk. He was questioning me beyond what was on the application but it didn't seem intrusive and I understood why he had to ask what he did. "How long have you been sober?" he asked me first.

"Off and on for three years but I had some slips. That's why I was up at High Ridge. I was an idiot and got a DUI and they gave me probation if I went to rehab. The state facilities were horror shows so I laid out the bucks and went to Kent."

"I have to ask you these things; don't take it the wrong way." He continued. "Remember this is a drug store; drug of choice – dope or booze?"

I shook my head. I had to come clean with him because I needed the job. "A little of both," I answered. "Basically, I got hurt ten years ago; terrible back pain and I got hooked on oxy. But I've been clean of that for three years. Stupidly, I lost everything and started drinking a bit too much. I was in Kent for three months. I got hired to work in the office and haven't had a drink in all that time."

Foster looked at me like he had heard all this a thousand times before and understood it all. "It is tough, addiction," he told me, "We all have our war stories. What did you do before?"

He was also easy to talk to and I knew he'd been through this procedure himself, so I answered him directly, "I sold software. I had a good job and made a lot of money. You must know how it is and how fast it can disappear."

He nodded with a knowing look in his eyes. "Tell me about it. I was an executive at IBM. They say you can never lose your job at IBM – not true if you're a drunk."

"My company let me go even though I was still doing all right selling." I told him.

"I've been sober now for fifteen years," he went on, "and manager here for the last eight. Opportunities are here at Rite-Aid if you want them."

"Thanks," I answered, "but right now all I want is just to survive. Maybe down the road, I'll think about the future. My whole past is gone, although I do have a grandson I'd love to meet."

He changed directions. "You're living at the Sojak house?" he said. "Be careful there. I've had my run-ins with Paulie. He's ripping the state off calling it a sober house so do watch your step." Getting back to business, he picked up the application papers, gave them one last look over and said to me officially. "Listen, the job is yours. It pays eight an hour but I'll up it to ten when you get by the two-week probationary period. That's the best I can do – keep you afloat. Do your job, you'll be fine."

I started the next day, exactly three days after moving into Paulie's place. It was easy boring work, stacking shelves, doing inventory and occasionally doing the cash register. It was tough with the low salary but Foster gave me enough hours so that I could pay my rent, buy food, fill my car with gas, and have a bit of running around money.

Over the years, both when I was a kid in school, and after I lost my software job, I worked many low paying jobs; construction gofer, sales clerk, paint store for my dad. I always consoled myself that it wasn't what I was going to do forever and I guess I always looked down my nose at the guys for which those jobs were a career. Right now, I was stuck with Rite-Aid but in my mind, it still wasn't my career.

For twenty-five years, from right out of college, I sold computer software. I did better than all right and made a good living. Back then I liked to live large; gamble, drink, spend money. My wife Connie made it easy for me to live like that. She liked the high life also; the nice house, the nice cars, the nice clothes, so she ignored my running around until I lost everything. On my part, I ignored her and ignored my kids and now I have nothing.

It's a strange thing about working minimum wage jobs. There's a certain personality of the people that have these jobs and if you don't fit this personality, the others resent you. Most of my life, I was successful and I had a good background. The other Rite-Aid workers picked up on this. Maybe I had an attitude; it's quite possible; I didn't want to be a stock clerk for the rest of my life.

Antoinette was the head cashier. An Italian woman in her early sixties, she had worked at that Rite-Aid for fifteen years and it was her life. I never said anything bad to her but she took an instant dislike to me. For a salesman, as I had been, that's a strange position, since we are always trying to charm people. I could only guess that Antoinette's dislike grew out of the feelings that I projected about the job.

"What are you doing working here, Cammond, slumming?" Antoinette asked me several times. Any time I tried to initiate some friendly conversation, she rebuffed me and her sentiments pretty much mirrored the feelings of some of the others in the store; especially those that had been there for quite a while. Foster, though, liked me. I was competent, learned quickly and in a short time, I could do everything in the store. After the probationary two weeks were over, he upped my pay to ten an hour and kept giving me more responsibility. He also started to encourage me to become a Pharmacy Tech. In reality that was a possibility; I was never going back to sales, but I wasn't interested.

"Donnie," Foster told me, "you can train right here in the store. It could be a new career for you." I couldn't envision myself at Rite-Aid for any lengthy period, although there were few other opportunities. I kept turning him down.

John Taylor was the assistant manager and he was an ass-kissing twenty-something-year-old who was looking for a career at Rite-Aid. He had started in that Rite-Aid as a high school student and worked there ever since. He was taking some college courses and it was clear that he expected to be a manager someday. He took Foster's encouragement of me as a threat to himself and thought that Foster was going to make me another assistant manager. Of course, it wasn't something I wanted, but to John Taylor, his job was everything and I scared him. He started constantly picking on my work. "Hey, Cammond, those shampoos you stacked aren't straight. Could you set them right?" And, "Cammond, don't make any mistakes at the register; fill your pockets. You understand me?"

A child threw up in one of the aisles and Taylor ordered me to clean it. I mopped it up and I was putting the mop away when Taylor started barking at me. "Cammond, can't you do anything right? There's still puke on the floor there." He dragged me back to the aisle and pointed at something, perhaps puke; it wasn't clear. "You better do it right now, Cammond." I'd had enough and I exploded. I grabbed his skinny frame by the shirt front and held him against the shelves. Antoinette looked on in horror. "You fucking little kid. Who do you think you're talking to? Keep talking to me like that and I'll throw your ass right through the front window."

He called the Stratford police and told them I threatened him. I smoothed it over with the cops and there was no arrest, but Taylor demanded that I be fired, and there wasn't much that Foster could do.

"Donnie," Ryan told me in a reluctant voice. "I have to let you go. He's claiming assault and it's best you don't fight this. If I hear of anything, I'll let you know."

With no job at Rite-Aid, I was right back where I started; living on the edge with no position, but I still didn't think of myself as a thin liner.

Four

"Donnie, what did you do before? You're a class guy and you don't fit in with us?" Mary asked me this several times, perhaps prompted by Paulie who was curious about my background. Coming from rehab, I learned that he had gotten the idea that I was an ex-con.

"I was a salesman," I told her. That and growing up in Bridgeport was all I told her although she kept asking. I felt it was better to be mysterious than to lay my life out in the open for these groups of grifters. Still, her asking me about my past, made me think about how I had gotten here. How did I wind up like this?

I've never been one to look backward, dwell on the past, or one to plan out the future. It's just not my personality. Most of the time, I plowed straight ahead, trusted my intuition and whatever happened, happened. For the first forty-five years of my life, just moving forward worked well for me.

We weren't poor when I was growing up and my mom did the books for my dad in his paint store. We lived in a nice house on a quiet street, around the corner from the store. It was not too different from Paulie's place. My brothers and I were in and out of that paint store throughout my childhood.

My dad was a serious dour Scots Presbyterian, although he never went to church. He kept to himself and never had much to do with us kids. Most evenings he worked in the store and when he did finally come home, he sat in his living room chair and read the newspaper or went directly to sleep.

He came to America as a teenager and when he spoke to us, it was either to bark orders, "Hey Donnie clean out the backroom," or to give advice, "Donnie you'd better buckle down and stay away from the thin line." He looked at everything in terms of paint and often said you could fix anything with a good covering. Never once do I remember a regular conversation with my father, and he ignored us in general. Still, he expected us to toe the line, stay out of trouble and do well in school. You learn what you see and unfortunately, I also had very little to do with my own children.

My mother, on the other hand, was a chatterbox Irish Catholic with deep auburn hair and blue eyes. I never thought of it as a younger man but she was a real looker. She ran the family and she and my dad were a strange couple, as strange as Paulie and Mary. They had three children but I can't recall ever hearing them have a conversation or saying a kind word to each other.

Down the street from the Sojak house was a Catholic church and I drove by it each day on my way home. They rang the church bells several times a day and you could hear them from Paulie's. I was talking to Mary in the kitchen when we heard the bells start to ring. She asked me, "Do you go to church Donnie?" She was almost childlike in her questions and easy to talk to, so I began opening up more to her than I would have liked.

"No," I told her, "I haven't been in church in years."

"I go occasionally, Easter and Christmas with my mother," she said. "Are you a Catholic?"

"Not really, well I guess sort of."

"What do you mean sort of?"

"My mother was a Catholic and she dragged my brothers and me to St. Ambrose every Sunday and we had to sit there and listen. Father Brendan would stand at the altar and boom out at the congregation; *you're all doomed to hell. All of you are sinners*."

Mary stared at me with her big doe eyes expecting me to say more. I went on. "Father Brendan was a joke, though, with his high-pitched girl's voice and little chubby body. Away from church, we used to laugh at him."

"I know the type," she told me. "My mother used to drag me to church also. My father never went. On Sundays, he went down to the Italian Club with his buddies to play cards. When I got to high school, I stopped going also. My mother would tell me – *you're going to hell Maria. You gotta keep your legs closed.*" Mary laughed.

"Yeah, my father never went either," I told her. "He sat at home and read when my mother dragged us to mass. He wasn't Catholic either. He was Presbyterian."

Mary looked at me with an odd look.

"Presbyterian," I told her, "that's just another church."

She nodded and despite trying to tell her as little as possible, I went on.

"Father Brendan wanted me to be an altar boy and my mother was delighted. My father wouldn't permit it though. No son of his was going to work in a Catholic church – sort of a holdover of how he felt in Scotland. My mother would yell at him – *'you're leading them away from heaven Peter'* – but my dad wouldn't budge. He never screamed back at my mom, just said a quiet no with his burr and that was that. It was a good move on his part. I heard that Father Brendan was too friendly with the altar boys, although back then, I was the type of kid who would have busted him up if he tried anything."

This last idea registered with Mary and she shook her head in a type of recognition. "In high school, I went to St. Bridget's, and Father Anthony, he was the Dean, he used to feel me up. I never said anything to anyone."

"Really. Why not?"

"I would get sent to his office when I got in trouble, smoking in the bathroom and such and he would say 'you should be a good girl, Mary,' and he would touch my tits – I was big then like now. He'd play with them a little and then send me back to class, tell me to be good. He never tried anything else, though, so I figured I was getting off easy, him touching my tits." She laughed.

"I guess you could look at it that way," I told her.

When I went to Bridgeport's Central High, I got to know all the Sojak and Mary types but they weren't my friends. I stayed on the good side of the school and hung out with the athletes and the serious students. I couldn't avoid knowing the thin liners though. Back then, the factories were closing down and industry in Bridgeport was drying up. The whole central industrial section, that had defined the city for over a hundred years, decayed. This left a big group from Central with no work to look forward to and no prospects, except to walk along that thin line. Twenty years earlier, this same group would have struggled through high school and then gone on to work at Bridgeport Brass or Remington Arms. With the union, they would have made enough to get married, buy a small house on the north end and spend Sundays drinking beer and watching football at Murphy's or Delaney's on Madison. For many on Bridgeport's North End, that was the definition of success. If you sat in Delaney's with your buddies on Sundays with a beer buzz and with all your bills paid, you knew you had made it. This group still drinks at the Bridgeport bars on Sundays, but now they're scrambling for the next buck in a city that has no work for them.

For my brothers and me, though, that was not the future. Ours was planned out; school, maybe college, job, family. My older brother, Mikey, was a football star at Central and could have gone to college. Instead, he married his high school sweetheart and became a Bridgeport cop. My dad liked his daughter-in-law but was not at all happy with his choice of the Bridgeport police. In the years when Mikey started, being with the Bridgeport PD was closer to being a criminal that any of the thin line walkers. The police commissioner and everyone down the line with the department were tied into the gangsters like Mara. Being on the take was expected. It was normal practice. I'm certain, or at least hopeful that Mikey stayed on the honest side of the thin line. He never got rich, put in his time with the department, bought a nice house down in

Black Rock, raised three boys, retired, and lives in Ocala where he fishes and plays golf.

My younger brother, Jamey, also played football and then went to work in the paint store with my mom and dad. My dad died when Jamey was thirty and he took over the store and ran it until the neighborhood changed and he couldn't make a living anymore. He then went into liquor sales and moved to Westchester, New York. He's been married and divorced twice, has a big booming laugh, and like me, never seems to look backward.

I also played football. I was the biggest of the brothers, and out of Central, I was a second-team all-state linebacker. I had some college offers, but I was also an excellent student. Mrs. Dundee, my high school counselor, found an academic scholarship for me to Montclair State College in New Jersey. I wanted to go into business and she told me that Montclair had an excellent business school. Playing football was okay, but studying just seemed better, so off I went to New Jersey, as much to get out of Bridgeport, as to get an education. At Montclair, I did all the right things. I majored in business and found a nice girlfriend, Connie Difrancesa. She was a Jersey girl from Caldwell, not too far from where we went to school. I studied and worked hard and married her right after graduation. I then got a job selling commercial software for a company in Jersey. For a long while, I left the whole Bridgeport world behind.

Five

So, what the hell was I doing here with Paulie Sojak, living out on the edge and flirting with walking the thin line? About ten years ago, everything fell apart. I guess it was my fault; whose fault could it be?

After graduation, my wife and I bought a house in Caldwell, near her folks. I was selling software, making good money and living well. I never thought much about any of my actions; I just skated along and rode the wave.

All the years that my mother dragged us to church, and all of Father Brendan's blustery sermons, made stealing, for me, out of the question. I was even straight with my income taxes and my account reports, unusual for a salesman with an open expense account. "Just pay them," I told myself, "they're my dues for living in a fair society."

All that financial honesty, though, made no impact on my concept of fidelity or on my domesticity. Like my father, I pretty much ignored my three children. I don't know if my dad ever regretted how he lived and treated us, but I do. Nothing slowed down my love of gambling or my eye for beautiful women. I had the money and I loved the high life. In Caldwell, among my neighbors, I was considered a solid family man, but I spent an awful lot of time in Atlantic City and up at Foxwoods. I loved the excitement of the casinos and I never thought much was wrong if I spent the night with some sweet young thing that I met at the crap tables or at a bar. My wife, Connie, was the perfect woman to enable me to live like that. She also loved the high life and took the money I made. We had a nice colonial on a full acre lot and she adored that nice house. She decorated it right out of her magazines. When I had it, she spent money like it meant nothing. We belonged to Caldwell Country Club, and she met with her friends and ignored it when I was gone. Connie was a good Italian homemaker, like her mother, who thought all men acted like me. Her father was a plumbing contractor in Caldwell, in business with his two sons, and Connie had grown up with them as her male role models.

Often, my father-in-law Ted was my companion at the casino. He was a gruff, barrel-chested man with a thick head of gray hair and a gray mustache, who shot craps enthusiastically and downed some scotch any time he could. At first, I was on my best behavior whenever I was with him. Then, one evening, we were at a bar at Mohegan Sun when he started talking to some young blonde, twenty years his junior. We were staying in separate rooms in the hotel and he winked at me and left with the girl. After that, I did what I wanted and we both looked the other way if we found some female company.

Then, I hurt my back. You wouldn't think a sore back could change a whole life, but it did. I can even picture the moment that it all started. I played racquetball at the Y three times a week and like everything in sports, I was intense and aggressive, always went full out when I competed. That night, I ran into the wall and something twisted and popped. I couldn't stand up and Ralph, my playing partner, had to help me to my feet. "Are you all right, Donnie?" he asked. I shook my head. I was in pain. "You'd better go home," he told me. I wanted to continue; it was against my competitive nature to just stop, but he was right, so I quit. At home, I iced it and did what the books tell you to do for a sore back, but it didn't heal. I was in agony. My regular doctor sent me to an orthopedist, who sent me to a surgeon, but nothing helped.

The surgeon, Dr. Carbone, told me, "Mr. Cammond, you have a badly pinched nerve. We call it spinal stenosis and all that can be done is to wait. I'm a surgeon but I have to tell you that the way the nerve is situated in your back, there is only a low chance that surgery will be successful. My advice is to go to physical therapy and then wait it out."

I waited and did the therapy but the pain was intense. I took ibuprofen and then Celebrex but I was in almost constant agony. I couldn't get comfortable at night and I went for several weeks without sleeping. Someone at work gave me oxycontin and those pills took the pain in my back away. It was as if, by magic, I could live normally again. Just the fact that I could sleep was a blessing.

In a heartbeat and without realizing it at first, I was hooked on the drug. Oxy is seductive, it's heroin after all. It's expensive and your body demands it. It's a pill and not messy like its brother heroin, so all that needle crap never intrudes. I hear that now people are taking heroin because they can't get oxy. However, oxy is strange; it affects everyone differently. For me, more than relieve the pain, the oxycontin caused me to exaggerate everything that I did. I gambled more than before, ran around more than before, and spent more money than before. Quickly, faster than I could imagine, I went through everything I had. First, I lost my job. I thought I was still doing all right and the drug hadn't affected my sales but Al Cafferty, the sales manager, called me into his office. I considered him a friend, but he was dead serious and not friendly when he sat me down across his desk from him. He had a cold look in his eyes when he told me, "Donnie, your behavior is erratic. I've told you that. You need help but I can't keep you on anymore. Do me a favor and please get the help."

I was certain that I wasn't hooked; the oxy was just to ease my back after all. "Come on, Al," I said, "I'm not hooked. I'm still pulling my weight, making my sales." He stood firm. "Don, you're out of control. I can't keep you on. I want to but I'm getting flak from upstairs. Please, please, as my friend get help."

"What are you, a fucking suck-up to Berman, Al? I'm still pulling my weight. I'm a producer. You know that. Come on, Al, we've been friends a long time."

He just shook his head. "Don, stay calm. Like I said, look at yourself, realize what's happening and get help. There's nothing I can do." He started looking at papers on his desk and I stalked out. I burnt my bridges and there was no going back. Without any cash rolling in, the oxy got even more expensive.

The bills started to pile up and the bank foreclosed on my mortgage. Connie took the kids to her parents and Ted also turned his back on me. I started having blackouts and week-long stretches would go by that I had no memory of what I did. Yet, the oxy kept calling me back and I answered the call. It took less than five years and I hit rock bottom; no home, no family, no real job. My back was too tender to handle any hard work, so I floundered from one small job to another. Nothing paid enough to keep up with my addiction. My brother, Jamey, had me selling liquor for his distributing company so I moved back to Connecticut. I managed to do that for a short while but I kept coming back to my drug of choice.

I'm not stupid. I knew what had happened but addiction is tough. That's a worn-out cliché but it's true. Just knowing that you've destroyed everything you had isn't enough. I had to do something more. I went to a few NA and AA meetings but I didn't think much of them and they had little effect on my addiction. I told my story and listened to the other war stories. I listened with half an ear; just a bunch of crybabies, I thought. The people I spoke to at the meetings told me that I always had the addictive personality; the gambling, the free spending, the womanizing. I didn't see it until the oxy grabbed me. Maybe that was true but knowing it didn't help me.

People who know me say that everything had come too easy for me; success in business, success in school and building a family. When I told my story at meetings, some comments were that I never appreciated what I had done. There I was though, hooked on oxy and with nothing left. Maybe I didn't appreciate all I had had but it was certainly gone. However, what people didn't realize is the strength of my own will power. Although everything seemed easy, it was really all planned out and followed from the force of my personality. The strength of my own will was what I had to fall back on.

I was working for my brother, Jamey, selling booze and living in Danbury in a rented room. The room was spare with nothing in it and at the time, it was about as far as I thought one could go from my big house in Caldwell. On a Saturday evening, I sat there alone and I was beginning to shake. I needed to score some oxy to calm down. The room was near Danbury Hospital and I knew a dealer who lived several blocks away. As I got up to leave, I spotted myself in the full-length mirror that had been hung by the front door. Instead of the large, muscular, athletic thirty-five-year-old that I still pictured myself as, the image was a gaunt, gray-haired, sixty-five-year-old. The man in the looking glass had the look of death about him. It startled me so I just stared and stared and then sat down. Was that figure really me? I stood up and looked again and the man in the mirror appeared even more like death. I sat back down and stayed in the apartment. Through sheer will power, I made it through that evening without oxy and made a vow to myself to stop using. Every addict has been at this point, at one time or another, but most vows fall by the wayside as soon as their drug of choice calls again. I was determined to keep mine. My huge ego had lied to me repeatedly and told me that I wasn't hooked, but of course, now I knew better. My huge ego would have to get me out.

The next evening, I went to my brother Jamey's house in Redding. He had gotten me work but he was always my baby brother and looked up to me. My addiction had shattered his view along with the other destruction it brought. Now, I needed his help more than ever. He was between wives and living alone; I sat him down and half crying and half slurring my words, told him that I was quitting oxy and asked him to sit with me.

"Donnie, I've heard all that before, what makes this time different?" he asked.

"Jamey, I want to live," I told him, never mentioning my image of death. "I don't know what's changed but I need to beat this. Listen, I've heard all the horror stories about withdrawal and I need your support. Sit with me and get me through at least a day or so. I'm certain I can take it from there. You know I always win."

"Donnie, you know I'll always do what's best for you. I have no experience with drug withdrawal but I'll do the best I can." His words were clear but he looked worried. Jamey was an alcoholic and fighting his own demons but as he sat there, he poured a good Scottish single malt for both of us. "Maybe booze will help get you through this, Donnie. It seems to work for me."

It didn't turn out as bad as I expected and I made it through four days, drug-free in his home. He sat by my side constantly and we talked and drank. As I was trying to beat my devil, we compensated with his. The conversations lasted for hours; from about my losses and my addiction to the ends of his marriages and his drinking. What we actually said has drifted away from me, drowned in the midst of fighting the oxy. At times, I felt very sick but surprisingly never unbearable. When the four days were over, I left Jamey's and then made it through another four on my own. I fought my way through the withdrawal and I was able to stop using. I never looked back and I never took another oxy. That was four years ago.

Other addicts have told me that what I did is impossible, oxy and heroin are just too strong, but I did it. Like everything else, I just plowed forward and suddenly my body stopped demanding it.

At first, the self-satisfaction of what I had done fueled my conceit and I thought I could get back my life but that wasn't the path that I was led to. Although, incredibly, my back stabilized, I had already slid too far downhill. I was in my mid-fifties, there was no real work for me and I was abandoned by everyone. My kids wouldn't talk to me and to my wife Connie, now broke herself; panhandling off her father and brothers, I was a pariah.

I was able to continue to sell liquor, store to store, but being around booze and drinkers made me start to drink a bit too much. When I felt the urge for the relaxed feel of the oxy, I would take a few drinks until I got a buzz. As with the oxy, I told myself that there was no problem. It was just the way I handled my "other problem" as I called it. My brother, Jamey, moved to Westchester and his company laid me off. I was back to nothing.

Three years ago, living in Danbury in that tiny furnished apartment and feeling sorry for myself, I stepped into a bar near Danbury Hospital and drank for an hour or two. Leaving there, I sideswiped a parked car, didn't stop, rode down the street and then passed out in the car. I was still sitting and dozing on the driver's side with the motor running when the Danbury police found me. Luckily, I killed no one, including myself, but I got a DUI and spent the night in jail. I was arraigned the next day in Danbury municipal court and at trial, the judge looked at my record and asked me, "Mr. Cammond, it's lucky you didn't kill someone. Do you have a drinking problem?"

I hung my head. Spending the night in jail was a sobering experience. The holding cells had a bunch of scuzzy-looking guys that gave me the evil eye. It was only that I was big and older that they left me alone.

"Yes, your honor," I answered him, "I guess I'm an alcoholic." I did not mention the oxy.

"You have no priors. I'm going to give you six months' probation if you go into rehab. Do you accept that?"

I knew that the state rehabs were horrible – almost like being in prison, so with the little cash I had left, I went to an AA run place, up near Kent, High Ridge Farm.

Six

One summer in high school, our football coach Mr. Jarrett had gotten the whole team jobs as the staff at Flagler's Hotel in the Catskills, somewhere near Ellenville, New York. My dad loved the idea. "Go off to a work camp son, it will be good for you," he told me as he signed the permission papers. The place Mr. Jarrett found, Flagler's, was a smaller Borscht Belt hotel like the one in the movie <u>Dirty Dancing</u> and that summer became one of the best of my teen years. I was a groundskeeper. I was out in the open air, worked about half a day, and played ball the rest. Mr. Jarrett ran a day camp for the premises, and in the late afternoons, he held football practice for us. In the evenings, we mixed with the hotel guests if we weren't working and I had my pick of pretty Jewish high school girls from New York City.

The rehab facility I went to reminded me of that hotel. It was built by a group affiliated with AA on what had once been a summer camp on the top of a mountain. The setting was idyllic; a lovely and serene location that at first glance gave the impression of a vacation spa. The appearance made it easy to sell the rehab to people scraping by, fighting their demons, and looking for the quick cure. Addiction isn't easy and the facility was smoke and mirrors; much more appearance than reality, although the staff diligently went through the motions. Each day, we attended several AA meetings and then discussions and classes. We had to share our stories and I told them about oxycontin but I left out how I had quit using. I was in rehab and I had to fit in, so I was a recovering addict just like every other patient. All of it might have worked if the people, both the addicts and the counselors, were really interested in making it work.

I found that most of the people in the rehab facility were thin liners and scammers. The majority were in rehab just to appease their families or the court system. It seemed that few were really there to get straight and become sober. "I'm having a drink as soon as I leave this place," was a line I heard quite often; just leaving the facility and returning to using seemed to be the mindset of the biggest bloc of patients. I felt bad for the others, those for whom there was a real dedication to stop. It would have been more effective for them if everyone had the same goal but unfortunately, that wasn't the case.

The younger people were mostly into narcotics, heroin, and coke. Many used the rehab to avoid jail time for selling. If you sold and you were wealthy and white, the court system could be persuaded to give you a chance at rehab. On the other hand, if you were poor and black and selling, it seems that the court system thought jail was best for you. Most of the younger patients were wealthy and the tortured faces of their parents on visiting day showed that money didn't shield a family from grief.

For the older people, some my age and some even older, the drug of choice was alcohol, although there were a few oxycontin users like me sprinkled in the mix. At the time, I learned that oxy was the fastest growing addiction although now, a few years later, maybe meth has passed it by. Most of the older people were established with careers and their addiction had destroyed everything, just as it had destroyed my life.

Listening to the stories that were shared at the meetings broke my heart. I stopped using by sheer will power, but I came to realize how bad a demon alcohol is. For most there, addiction was coupled with depression and they self-medicated with booze. This led to being drunk which led to more depression in what seemed to be for them an endless cycle. The myth is that one goes to rehab and gets sober but that is just a myth. Addiction, alcohol or drugs or even gambling or sex, is just too tough and the quick recovery almost never happens. Some of the people I met at High Ridge were in rehab over twenty times. One poor fellow, a surgeon from Yale New Haven, ran away one evening and they found him dead in a motel in New Milford. His room was littered with empty vodka bottles; he drank himself to death.

Many of the AA methods might be successful; twelve step programs seem to be the only thing that works for hardened users, but at High Ridge most of the methods were just bullshit for the scammers. They were going through the motions. They told their horror stories convincingly enough at meetings, and their desire to quit seemed real, until I spoke to them during the free times. "Yeah I want to quit but shit, I have it all under control," one young fellow from Manhattan told me. "My folks found my stash and they sent me up here or they would've thrown me out. I'll have to be more careful when this is done."

For me though, the time I spent at that rehab wasn't bad at all. The women were willing, so it became a month of listening to people's woes, trying to be empathetic, and then bedding emotionally wounded females. For many, sex was a medication that came without the penalties of booze or dope, and they needed the warmth of another human being. I had a sympathetic ear and a warm body and that was all I needed. We stayed in dorms, much like camp dorms with two or more per room. Mixed sex fraternization was forbidden and if patients were caught having sex, they were to be thrown out. However, this was adults with addiction needs and sex was rampant. I spent a lot of my down time in the women's rooms. Mostly, it was sex with no ties. I needed the human contact as much as my partners and I hardly remember the names of most of the women I bedded.

Seven

Elena McCann was the director of the facility. In her early fifties and herself a recovering alcoholic, she wasn't bad looking, but she had the drawn tight face and the gin-soaked baritone of a heavy drinker. I learned that she had sobered up at High Ridge twenty years earlier and had slowly worked herself into the director's position and a prominent position on the Board of Directors. The other Board members, most recovering addicts themselves, thought she was the sun and the moon and left everything about the facility to her.

I met Elena at the initial intake. I paid for three weeks, the minimum that the court order required. Like Paulie had done, when I moved into his house, she said all the right things at the first interview.

"Mr. Cammond, as you know addiction is difficult. However, if you follow the methods we outline, we feel that there is a good success rate. Many of our alumni continue on their sobriety."

She was quite convincing and I nodded. Perhaps she was correct but I felt that I had defeated the demon that was oxy, and alcohol was just an annoyance. I'd put in my three weeks and leave, go back to the meager life that I had fallen into.

Elena interviewed each patient and his or her family, if there was any, at their arrival. As she did with me, she explained the rules and the program. She was an excellent salesman and made the quick recovery seem possible. She didn't lie about it and said that it was a tough process, but she was upbeat enough, so that families and those patients that really wanted it came to believe. It was only after being there a while that the rosy picture began to muddy.

It did not take me long to realize that Elena was a scam artist, another thin liner. She had complete control of the facility's finances and I'm certain that she was stealing. Her husband was a retired attorney from Hartford and their home was a beautiful contemporary house near the facility. They had another place in Quogue on Long Island and they lived way beyond what a director of this type of facility could earn. Her husband, Ed, was senile and most afternoons he spent at the farm sitting alone silently on a bench.

Elena ruled High Ridge with an iron fist; the staff and counselors all tiptoed around her. If she liked you, it was a good place to work but if she didn't, and her moods changed constantly, you were out the door quickly.

After the initial intake, she didn't interact that much with the temporary patients but she took a liking to me and I became, what the other staff behind her back called "Elena's flavor of the month". It was near the end of my three-week paid rehab that she called me into her office for an *evaluation*. She sat at her desk and I sat facing her. It began as something quite official. "How is everything going, Don? Have you gotten into the swing of the program? Has it helped?" she asked me.

"It's okay, Ms. McCann," I told her. I just wanted to fulfill the court order and I wanted no trouble.

"You can call me Elena," she said and smiled at me. "We want you to be comfortable here. When you relax and go with what we're trying to do, the program can become effective. I've heard from the counselors that you were an oxycontin user as well as a drinker. You never mentioned that on your application."

Her eyes were flirting with mine and I realized that this was more than just an evaluation. I decided to play along and see where it led. "I stopped using oxycontin three years ago, really, but I developed a problem with alcohol also. That's why I came here – for the alcohol."

"We all have all sorts of problems," she told me. "That's why we're here." She stood up and walked by me and closed her office door. She then walked back and stood by my chair and suddenly stroked my cheek. "You have no family, Don? No one's come to visit." She then slowly massaged my shoulders.

"They don't want me. You must know how it is," I answered.

She leaned down and kissed me gently. "It gets lonely, doesn't it?" she whispered and then kissed me more deeply. I slipped my hand onto her behind and pulled her onto my lap. She was willing and fell easily into my arms. We made out a bit on that chair and then I did her, right on her office couch, with the door barely closed and with most of our clothes still on. She wasn't bad, but her body had the feel of a woman that had had a thousand lovers and sex was just an exercise, an important exercise but just that.

She straightened herself up a bit and then went back to her desk. "Don, would you like to work here after your rehab is done? We call it an extended stay. It's nonpaying but you get your room and board and the therapy. You can also come and go as you please."

"Elena, I'm almost broke, so without any pay I can't come and go at all, but I like the idea," I answered her.

"If I can get you some money, say two hundred a week, would you stay?"

"If you can do that, I'll stay. What will I do?"

"I'll put you at the front desk, answering phones, going over paperwork. Does that sound okay?"

After the paid-for rehab was over, I began this extended stay position, working the front desk and being a part-time diversion for Elena. While her poor, clueless husband sat in his senile state on the property, she'd ferry me to her house during lunchtime for nice sandwiches and a nooner. I certainly wasn't the first doing all of this, nor was I the only one at this time; one evening, I spotted her walking out of the chapel with another staffer. I didn't mind; this was just another bus stop on the road to who knew where.

It took about six weeks, but I guess I wore out my charm. I made some silly mistake with the mail and she blew up at me, "Cammond, you're worthless here. I'm putting you in the kitchen. No forget it, you're out of here."

She made me leave. I packed up the little stuff that I accumulated and put it into my car and then I was right back to scrambling. However, the time I put in at the facility cleansed my court record and I was able to drive.

Lucille Cartman, the assistant director, gave me the address of the Sojak sober house in Stratford and gave me the lead to Ryan Foster and to Rite-Aid. Lucille was also a recovering alcoholic who had stayed on working in the office and worked her way up to assistant director. She was a straight arrow and the antidote to Elena. She took the job of getting people to recover seriously, and was one of the staff that really cared. She did her best also to please Elena and protect herself, but she felt bad that Elena fired me. "Donnie, I'm sorry that she let you go. It's not your fault, you lasted longer than most."

Lucille waved goodbye as I drove off of the farm and headed to the Sojak house. After all these years, I was back in the Bridgeport area but I was fifty-eight years old, with no real job, no real prospects and no chance of getting anything.

Despite everything, and after ten years of living on the edge, I still had my nose in the air and looked down at the scammers like Paulie and Elena and the idiots like Mary. I believed that I was better than them. Even after all this time rolling downhill, I expected it to turn around. I called it my rosy outlook and through everything, it had kept me going.

Eight

After losing my job at Rite-Aid, I sat for two whole days in Paulie's house just reading and trying not to think about what I would do. It was difficult to contemplate. Paulie and Mary were in and out of the house and probably wondered why I wasn't at work but I said nothing. Eventually, I had to face the obvious truth that the rent money would dry up and I had to find some work, some source of income. I called Foster and asked if he had heard of anything.

"There's an opening at Walgreen's further down the Post Road. With the experience you had here, you might get it." He told me this but he was rather cold and didn't seem encouraging.

I went to the Walgreen's and filled out the application. I stood around and finally got to talk to the manager. He was my age, like Foster, heavyset and bald, and he looked over my application and then looked at me. "You're the guy who beat up John Taylor at Rite-Aid, right?"

I nodded. There was no point trying to hide that.

"He's a prick," he told me. "I know him and I can see how he'd fire you up but I can't hire you. You know that, right? Good luck though."

I nodded and walked away. Near the counter, I spotted a yellow plastic bat and ball, ages three to five. I bought it for three ninety-five. I shouldn't have been wasting what little money I had, but maybe I could give it to Gene one day. I put it on the back seat of my car.

I tried to get a job as a barista at a Starbucks but they only took my application; the same at Wal-Mart. I'd fill out an application and they'd say, "we'll get back to you." If I called back, they'd say we haven't made a decision yet. I guess my job applications, with the lapses between jobs and the many different jobs, signaled something wrong – addiction or at least a problem. On top of that, most of them seemed to look unkindly at my age. If I was already on Social Security, I got the impression that it might have been easier, but I was at a very awkward age; too young to retire and too old to get anything new.

The next two weeks, I tried my best, following up every lead I could find; word of mouth, newspaper ads and help wanted signs. I started to know every store along the Post Road in Stratford and over the bridge into Milford. It was two weeks of constant rejection and the frustration level was incredible. Every "no" began to hit me harder and soon each rejection was accompanied by an actual physical pain that came out of nowhere. Maybe my life, even with losing everything had been too easy; maybe now I was really at rock bottom and what I thought had been bad before was really a step upwards. I had listened to so many war stories, especially of the older people at the rehab. Secretly, when I heard them, I thought, "Just get up off the floor. Don't be a fucking whiner." Maybe I was arriving at where they had been.

I spoke to a luncheonette owner about a counter job. He looked to be about my age and I thought we hit it off well. He said he'd let me know. I called him back and he said he decided not to hire but I noticed that the want ad was still up in his window. Some days later, it was down and I went in and found a good-looking young woman working behind the counter. He spotted me but wouldn't look at me; I was pissed and completely frustrated and I stalked out.

There was a liquor store next door to the café and I went in, and in a fit of anger, bought a pint of Dewar's. What the fuck good was staying straight doing me anyway?

I sat down on the front seat of my car and unscrewed the top. I was going to take a swig in the car but a Stratford police car drove by and I caught myself. "Fuck it," I told myself, "drink it at home then just go to sleep. Don't make things even worse." Even at my lowest moments, I still had some wits about me. I screwed the cap back on and drove to Paulie's.

I pulled into the side driveway where I usually parked. Paulie had a big parking area that fit three or four cars. I sat a while in the driver's seat and took a good look at the Sojak house. "What a fucking dump." I hung my head, then picked up the unopened Dewar's and started to go inside. I spotted the yellow plastic bat I had bought sitting on the rear seat so I leaned over and picked that up also. I went through the back door into the kitchen. No one was there. I put the bottle and the bat on the dining room table and poured myself a glass of water for a chaser. Then I took the cap off of the bottle again. My hands were shaking.

"Don't be a forking chump, Donny," I could almost hear my father say. "You're a tougher lad than this and it will all pass." I put the bottle on the table and went to the fridge. I was hungry. I found a half can of soup that I had left over from the night before and heated it on the stove. I put it in a bowl and sat back down. I took a spoonful and a sip of water and then reached with my shaky hand for the bottle. I pulled my hand away and looked at the pint. Maybe, just maybe, I could white-knuckle this and get through it without drinking. I put the spoon down and held my head in my hands and covered my eyes.

Finally, I looked up again and stared at the bottle. Sitting alone at that table with the half-eaten bowl of soup and the open scotch, everything hit me at once. From a place deep inside my memory that I hadn't opened in ages, I started to picture the big Thanksgiving dinners at my in-laws; four grown children and all their kids; pasta, turkey, wine, laughing. If I could just have one more fucking Thanksgiving, one fucking Thanksgiving where I could smile and my kids would call me something other than asshole. One fucking nice dinner where little Gene, my grandson, would sit on my lap. My eyes started to tear and I wiped them. I knew I had fucked everything up. That was old news, but now that old news was pounding me like a hammer, hitting my body and my head repeatedly.

Then just as suddenly as I pictured Thanksgiving, I remembered the sad last time I had seen any of them. Our big, beautiful house that Connie had decorated so exquisitely had been sold at foreclosure, and she was living at her folks with my youngest, my daughter Gina. I went into the house to get the last of my stuff. It was supposed to be shipped to me and I was forbidden to be there but I wanted one last look. In the kitchen, I downed an oxy to feel better and then mellowed out and slumped into my old chair. Don Jr., my oldest son, twenty-seven at that point, walked in and saw me.

"What are you doing here?" he barked. "You know you're not supposed to be in this house."

I pulled myself to my feet and looked at him. "Don't talk to me like that. Show me some respect, I'm your father."

"You're a fucking junkie," he snarled. "Why should I show you any respect?"

We stood eye to eye and I realized that there was nothing I could do. He was bigger than I was, six-four, to my six-three, and he weighed at least two fifty. He never finished college because I didn't have the money to pay for the tuition and he was working in the plumbing business with his grandfather and his uncles. Although I still viewed myself as a big tough guy, I realized he could kick my ass. Besides, I couldn't physically fight with my son no matter what he said. I fell back into the chair. He gave me a cruel look of contempt.

"Just don't be here when I get back," he said and left.

"What a fucking jerk I was," I said to myself. I sat some more in Paulie's kitchen, the open bottle on the table, the half-eaten soup right in front of me, and I started to really cry. I tried to stop. "It will all pass, laddie," my father's words kept saying to me.

All this mental wrestling exhausted me and I fell asleep sitting there. I woke up to Mary's hands on my face.

"Are you all right?" Mary asked. She held my face and I liked the warmth that her body gave off. Paulie stood by the sink and I saw he was holding my pint of Dewar's and the cap was back on.

"Were you drinking in here, Donnie?" Paulie asked. He tried to be tough but when I gave him a hard look and told him "no," his tone softened. "Just don't drink right in the open – you know it's bad for the house."

I turned to Mary, "I'm just exhausted." She held me to her chest like I was child. "You know we'll look out for you." I spotted Paulie staring and there was a hint of jealousy in his eyes. "Thanks Mary. Thanks, Paulie." I told them. I stood up, then noticed the yellow bat and ball on the table. I picked it up, nodded at Mary and then at Paulie, and carried it upstairs to my room. I placed it on top of the dresser, next to Gene's picture, lay down and quickly fell asleep.

Nine

I slept solidly for eight hours and when I woke, I had a headache as if I had been drunk. I lay in bed, awake, for quite a while, thinking. "It's better that I hadn't downed the scotch," I thought to myself. Sitting in that kitchen, the world had caved in around me, but the sleep had pushed it all back inside me. My natural outlook returned. None of this was really easy for me but I always pushed forward, one foot ahead of the other. "I'll do what I have to do."

Lying there, I realized that I had nowhere to turn except to Paulie. I hated to do it, deal with a thin liner, but he had told me he knew of a job and, like being here in the first place, what else could I do. I checked my watch. It was before seven and I knew that Paulie hadn't left yet for work, so I walked down to the kitchen and made some coffee. Ten minutes later, he walked out of the bedroom, part of his morning routine. He had on his pants and work shoes but only a tee shirt. He looked over at me and nodded.

"Do you want some coffee, Paulie. I made some."

"Sure, Donnie, thanks." He said nothing about the previous night.

I poured a cup and handed it to him and then sat down at the table. He put in some sugar and sat down across from me.

"Thank you for not blowing up last night," I said. "I was out of line with the bottle. I was really pretty low."

"Forget it, Donnie. If you didn't drink, there's no problem, no foul. I understand."

I had to ask him about work, so I bit the bullet and asked. "Paulie, I'm finished at Rite-Aid, couldn't stand it. Do you know of anything?"

"I heard about Rite-Aid through the grapevine. They say you threatened to throw that Johnny Taylor through the window." He nodded and seemed to smile at that. "You can't find nothing else? That must have been a week and a half ago."

He clearly liked the idea of me being a tough guy. It fit in with his mistaken perception that I was an ex-con. I was embarrassed by my actions in Rite-Aid. I never should have blown up like that, but I didn't want to show this to Sojak.

"He was an asshole," I answered. "He deserved it but now I need a job. I've been beating my head against a wall. There's nothing out there for a guy my age. Scumbag at the café off the green has a help wanted sign out and he wouldn't hire me."

Paulie relished the fact that I was asking him for help. Scammers always like when others owe them favors. "Sure, Donnie I can get something for you. Goat has a business you know, and he needs someone in the office. I think you'd be perfect there."

Paulie was a scammer but a decent sort and he and I got along. Just as Mary had this strange crush on me, Paulie also seemed to look up to me. He was an odd fellow and sometimes it seemed like he believed that he was running a legitimate sober house. "Don," he told me "I should bring the hammer down on Eddie McGuire. I know he's popping pills and I should throw him out, but where the hell is he going to go? I wish I could get him to stop. It looks bad for me with the town, to have these users here." He seemed genuinely concerned. Whether it was for poor Eddie McGuire, or for the way it looked with the town, I couldn't tell. In the end, though, he did nothing and let McGuire continue to stay.

I met some of Paulie and Mary's crowd, like Paulie's best friend Goat, who came in and out of the house and helped himself to anything he found in the fridge. I found that I was adjusting to the environment; I hated drifting toward the thin line section but it was happening. Despite my nose in the air attitude, it was easy to talk to Paulie and Goat and Mary and they appeared to accept me. If I was going to work for Goat, I'd have to just get used to it.

Ten

Goat Errico was Paulie's scam partner as well as his closest friend. The name on his business cards was Gabriel but everyone knew him as Goat. I never learned where the nickname came from and never asked; just called him Goat and let it go at that. He ran a business selling and installing electric generators in private homes and he started me working in the office, taking orders and scheduling installations. Paulie warned me, even though Goat was his pal. "Get paid each week up front Donnie. Don't let Goat rip you off."

Goat was single and lived in an old two-story private house. It hadn't been painted recently and was a step down from the Sojak place. It was only several streets from Paulie's but I still drove there every day. The business office where I worked was on the ground floor and his apartment was upstairs. He had a separate, small office for himself just behind mine. He kept his inventory and his tools in a back garage. He had no other regular employees and if he needed help on installations, he hired workers as needed and paid them on a cash basis.

The front door opened to the business office so he had to come in and out that way. I saw him constantly. Some days, he'd be gone all day; other days, he stayed by himself on the second floor and watched television. Every so often, he'd go through papers in his working office. Often, Paulie would stop by for coffee and he and Goat would disappear upstairs and plan out whatever scheme they were into.

Goat was about Paulie's age, same size and build, and sort of nondescript. He had a contractor look and he was not a bad salesman. Power outages were becoming common and private home generators were more and more in demand. Besides selling generators, he did some electrical work.

A few days in the office and I knew his business was a sham. For every three orders we took, he installed maybe one generator but collected money on all three. There were constant complaints that I had to field. That was my real job, placating angry customers. "Oh, we're just busy now. We'll be out there to finish the job next week." I said that so often, I got sick of it. Despite the never-ending complaints, he managed to juggle the customers and do just enough work to keep the business going.

As the point man in Goat's office, I replaced Angelos Papajohn. Goat and Paulie referred to him as Nick the Greek or just the Greek and spoke about him quite a bit.

"Look, Donnie," Goat ordered me, "if this fat Greek comes in here looking for me, you don't know where I am. Don't let him hang out here either. Get rid of him."

Angelos was an overweight, disbarred lawyer, who I learned had fleeced the whole Greek community in Bridgeport. Goat filled in the details on the whole story, or at least the parts that made Papajohn look bad. Father

Costa, a priest at St. John the Archangel, realized that Papajohn was cooking the church books and went to the police. Angelos was indicted and went to trial. He was tied in to the Bridgeport political machine and he beat jail time but Father Costa was tenacious and wouldn't give up. He filed a complaint with the state bar association and eventually Papajohn was disbarred. Goat gave him the job of doing the books, taxes and legal work and running the office. If Goat needed some official legal work, Papajohn had a young cousin, Tom Panos, another lawyer, who handled it. Panos was incompetent and Papajohn would have to do the actual work. When it was completed, Panos would simply sign off on it.

At one point, the Greek gave Goat his American Express Card to keep Goat's business running. It was impossible to tell where Goat's cash disappeared to, but he was always crying poverty and was constantly cash poor. Goat ran up the Greek's charge card. The bill went to Papajohn and Errico avoided paying him back. Goat was a thin-liner to the core.

At least once a week, Papajohn came to the office and tried to collect the money that was owed to him from the card. Goat somehow had a sixth sense and was out of the office whenever the Greek showed up. Angelos wore tailored, expensive clothes, but nothing fit him and he constantly looked unkempt; shirt out with his huge stomach hanging over his belt line. He always wore a tie but his neck folded over the shirt collar. On warm days, he sweated like a sieve. At first, I tried to follow Goat's orders and shoo the Greek out of the office. "Look, Mr.

Papajohn," I told him "Goat is away until tomorrow. There's no point you hanging out here."

Angelos ignored what I said and sat at the desk and talked. "Look Cammond or Donnie, or whatever, I know Goat is ducking me. I'm going to keep coming here until I get my fucking money. He owes it to me; he's going to give it to me."

When he finally found Goat in the office, though, he wasn't very forceful. He tried to be tough. I stayed to the side and listened.

"Where's my fucking money, Goat, you ran up the card and I had to pay it."

"Look, Angie, you know I'm good for it," Goat told him. "I'm just waiting for a few orders to come through. You know I'll throw you some stuff here and there."

"Well, you better," Angelos said, trying to browbeat him, but it was clear that the Greek's threats had no bite.

After that, Papajohn still came in almost every day to the office. He told me that he still handled some of the tax preparation. If Goat wasn't there, he talked to me. He was a bit younger than I, and he found out, from either Paulie or Goat, that I grew up in Bridgeport. He talked to me about the old days in the city.

"Yeah Don, back then everything was wide open and a man could make a bundle," he told me. He sipped a hot cup of coffee and was sweating as he sat across from me at my desk. His expensive but ill-fitting suit was soaked. "It was easier then, not so much oversight; state panels and shit." He knew all the politicos, as he called them, and all the police bigwigs, and was still hooked into anything underhanded in the Greek community. "If I got in a jam back then, it would disappear quickly; know what I mean?" He then asked me. "Where did you live, Don?"

I told him, "My Dad owned a paint store on Madison and we lived a block away."

"That's right, Cammond's. I knew the place. I used to go by it all the time; never met your Dad, though. I never did much painting," he chuckled at that and his neck jiggled as he laughed. "Easier to hire someone."

He complained to me about Goat and the others, but the fact that Goat had stolen from him didn't seem all that upsetting to him. Scammers and thin liners think everyone else is just like them and getting ripped off in the process of trying to rip someone else off is just part of the lifestyle. I started calling him Angelo like he was my friend.

I found myself drifting towards the thin line. I didn't want to, but it was just happening. When you're scraping to get by, any few dollars are important. I wasn't scamming, myself, I hadn't stooped to that yet, but I turned a blind eye to whatever Goat, Paulie, Angelo and the bunch scammed. I rationalized it by saying, "I'm not doing anything. What they do is their business." However, living by yourself becomes lonely and I began to hang out with Paulie, Mary and Goat and their crowd.

Eleven

Paulie and I were friendly but I tried to keep my distance. I talked to him quite a bit; he told me about some of his scams – he never referred to them that way – but they were scams just the same. I listened, nodded my head and didn't say too much. The fact that I never reproached him encouraged him to tell me even more.

"Donnie," he started one evening, "don't be alarmed if you hear some noise this evening. I'm doing some business with Louie Barzino, the landscaper."

I nodded and said "okay" and nothing more. He could have left it at that but it was as if he wanted to tell me what he was doing. He was proud of his little plot.

"Barzino's buying gas from me for his lawnmowers and trimmers and such. I have an open account for my city truck and no one ever checks on it. Why not get a few bucks, eh Donnie?"

Again, I nodded. The fact that I said nothing made me feel complicitous and I didn't like the feeling, but what else could I say? I was living in Paulie's world, working for his friend, and talking quite a bit with his girlfriend. This was my life as it stood and I had to keep it moving.

I'm certain Paulie was a bit afraid of me. I was still big, and coming from rehab, he got the idea that I might be an ex-con. I had learned from Goat that over the years several convicted drug offenders had lived in Paulie's sober house. Whatever the reason, he stepped ever so gingerly around me. I never told him anything. I felt it was better for him to be a bit wary of me than to be too familiar.

Mary, though, had this crush on me. I'm certain of it. Whenever Paulie was gone, and I was in the house, she would sit by me and talk. She told me all about school, her parents and her background. She looked at me with her big brown eyes and I knew that all I had to do was ask her and I could take her upstairs to bed. Here again, what could I do? She was Paulie's girlfriend and I really didn't want to screw up my living arrangements when I had nothing else to fall back on.

One evening, I was reading at the dining room table when Mary came flying out of their bedroom. Paulie stormed out after her screaming, "You stupid, pothead whore," and then knocked her down. "Get your fucking ass back to your parents," Paulie spit out as he stood over her.

Mary was crying and lying on the floor covering her head. Paulie went to hit her again and I grabbed him by the arm. "Hey Paulie, just back off," I told him and gave him a hard but firm stare. I then pulled him backwards while Mary scrambled to her feet. Paulie looked at me and said nothing. If he had fought with me, I don't think my back would have held up, but luckily, he backed off. Mary stood by the rear door that went out to the small back deck, still crying and Paulie stared over at her. He then walked back into the bedroom. Mary walked outside to do a joint and cry some more.

After stopping Paulie from beating her, Mary's crush on me grew. Two times when Paulie and Goat were out, I went with her to dinner over at a diner in East Haven. "I'll pay, Donnie," she told me "I love to talk to you."

She and Paulie were always on and off, but he let her stay. They'd break up and she went back to her parents for a few hours and then she'd be back. There was constant screaming between them, mixed in with noisy lovemaking. The walls in the house were paper thin and I could hear everything.

Her folks, Italian immigrants, lived on the other side of Stratford. They weren't rich, her father was a stone worker and mason who had built a good private business. Mary grew up, solidly lower middle-class; typical Stratford girlhood. She started doing drugs and booze in high school and she'd been in trouble since ninth grade. She went on to community college but eventually her parents threw her out. They still paid for her school and helped her out occasionally. I met her mother at Paulie's house when Mrs. Furillo brought her some clothes and some home cooked food. Her mother was an old-fashioned Italian, like my ex-mother-in-law, and you could hear the confusion in her voice when she talked about Mary. It was inconceivable to her that Mary wasn't finding a husband and settling down. "Mr. Cammond," she said to me in a thick Italian accent "Mary at thisa age she shoulda be more settled, married or at least outta school. I donna know what to do."

Her folks liked Paulie because he took care of her. They wanted Paulie to marry her. "Mr. Cammond," she continued, "Mary shoulda marry Paulie. He's a nicea guy, takes care of her, and owns his owna house." In my mind, I wanted to tell her that Paulie was just a low-life scammer but the poor woman needed something to believe in.

Mary, slow as she was, thought of herself as an intellectual; after all she was in college and she liked talking to me. I knew books and I knew movies and I read the New York Times. I guess I was a step up from the other guys in her life.

The house phone rang one evening and I answered it. It was Mary. She was hysterical and sobbing, "Where's Paulie? I need Paulie," she wept.

"What's going on?" I asked her. "Paulie's not here."

"What am I going to do, Donnie. They're holding me at Bridgeport Correctional. Can you bail me out? I can't stay in here."

Some weeks before, she had gotten a DUI and never answered the court date. That evening, she had gotten drunk and picked up by the Bridgeport PD. With Paulie out somewhere, I went down to Bridgeport, paid the bail and took her back to the Sojak house. The court system doesn't look kindly on missed court dates and she was looking at real jail time. She sobbed during the whole ride to Stratford. Once back in the house, Paulie still wasn't there, she put her head on my shoulder and hugged me. "Thank you, Donnie, you're my angel, my savior." She repeated that two or three times and then kissed me. I kissed her back but I felt nothing. Her wasted look was a turn off for me. She was moving her body next to mine and I had to stop her. "Mary," I told her, "You're Paulie's girlfriend. I can't do any more. It's just not right."

She pulled away but she looked at me with her big doe eyes and said, "Donnie, please let me thank you. You were so sweet to come and get me. Let me give you head. I'm great at it." It was hard to refuse an offer like that, so I let her go down on me while I sat in my usual kitchen chair. It was okay, but all the time I expected Paulie to walk in; really dampened the mood. After that evening, though, whenever Paulie would slap her around, or they had a big blowout, she found a way to sneak into my room and go down on me – just the way it was.

Twelve

Some nights in that old smelly house, my head would feel like it was about to explode. My room was tiny and as I grew anxious, the whole place seemed to close in on me. I had nowhere to go but I had to get out so I'd go for a drive. One night, I went over to my old neighborhood just to see what it looked like and how much it had changed. It was mostly black now but the houses and stores looked the same. My dad's store was gone and it had become some sort of small market. There were a bunch of guys hanging out in front drinking beer.

I went over to Delaney's, three blocks south, and went in and sat at the bar. I was going to have a beer, then thought better of it and had a diet coke. Delaney's was a straight up old-fashioned shot and beer place and the bartender gave me a strange look when I asked for the soda. If one wasn't going to drink, a neighborhood tavern on the north end of Bridgeport was not the place to go into.

An older fellow with white hair and a beat-up red-veined drinker's face came over to me. He was smiling.

"Donnie Cammond? Is that you? I ain't seen you in forty years."

I had no idea who he was and I guess my lost look gave me away.

"It's me, Nicky Pinto from Central. We played ball together. Don't you remember? What you been up to?"

He looked like hell and never in a hundred years would I have recognized him. He looked seventy-five. I had no idea what I looked like to him, but seeing him and realizing that we were contemporaries aged me quickly in my mind.

"Nicky. Sure, I remember; tough to pick you out after all these years," I lied. "I'm just scraping by. I live in Stratford."

"Me too, just scraping by," he told me. "I haven't worked in fifteen years since I lost my job at the Brass. But I get by, still live with my mom in the same house. Don't need much. Your Dad's store is gone. I used to see your brother Mikey around but I ain't seen him in a while either. Did he retire?"

"Yes," I told him, "he moved down to Florida."

Nicky nodded and paused like he wanted to say more but couldn't think of anything. He looked over at the people he had been drinking with and then back at me. "Well, Donnie, stop in more often. Don't be a stranger."

He walked away and I left. I had to shake my head in the car as I drove back to Stratford. It was sad to think that this is where I was.

Nostalgia really isn't my thing and I didn't return to the old neighborhood but I drove other places. I went up to New Haven to have a pizza at Pepe's and then down to Port Chester in New York to a bar we used to frequent. Back then, the drinking age in Connecticut was twenty-one but it was eighteen in New York. Summers during my college years, a bunch of us would drive the thirty miles to Port Chester to drink. It probably wasn't the safest thing but at nineteen, getting drunk was more important than safety.

Then I realized that I couldn't really afford the gas to be cruising all over. I tried taking a walk, but even though I had been a good athlete, I hate just walking, so it was back to Paulie's kitchen.

When Paulie wasn't around and Mary was, she sat and talked to me. After bailing her out and our little evening together, her crush was even stronger. Often, I felt so lonely, I wanted to take her upstairs to my room and screw the hell out of her, just to feel a warm body next to mine. If I knew Paulie would be gone for a few hours, I had her give me head, she never turned me down. I still drew the line at that with Mary. It may seem crazy but I still couldn't do more with her. She'd kiss me and I'd push her away and she'd give me a pained look like "what did I do wrong?" "Mary" I'd tell her, "I've never been one to knowingly screw around with someone else's girlfriend. You're sweet but I can't do more." Still, I let her go down on me when I was confident Paulie would be gone. After I'd finish, I'd shake my head and tell myself that I was starting to act just like the thin liners around me, but I kept doing it.

Thursday evenings, Paulie and Mary met some of their other friends at the AMX Bowling Lanes in Milford. There was a bar with a juke box and a dance floor attached to the alleys and Paulie and Mary knew many of the people that hung out there. One evening, they invited me to go along.

For me, it became a way to kill time. I wasn't much of a bowler, never was, but going there and socializing was better than sitting and reading in Paulie's kitchen. At the bowling lanes, I met Diamond Bramble.

Diamond was a thin, balding fellow with outsized muscular arms. We were sitting at a lane finishing up when he walked over to us. He had on a janitor's uniform and he glanced at me with a quizzical look and then spoke to Paulie, "How are you doing, Paulie? Who's the new guy?" Paulie was tallying our bowling scores and glanced up from the sheet. He smiled at the skinny fellow. "Hey Diamond, where you been?"

"Just here and there," the fellow answered and then Paulie nodded at me. "Donnie, this is Diamond Bramble, a friend of mine. Diamond, this is Donnie Cammond. He lives at my place and he works for Goat."

I looked at the fellow. He was twitchy and couldn't look directly back at me. I held out my hand and joked, "Diamond Bramble. Is that your real name?" He shook my hand and nodded, "Sure what's wrong with it?" as if it was the most common name around.

It was Bramble who introduced me to Holly and I came to blame him for finally tipping me over the line. In truth he was just a guy, another scammer, and anything I did, like everything I had done before, was my own fault.

Bramble, despite the muscled arms that caught your eye immediately, was scrawny and ugly, with a pockmarked face and a shaved head. He wasn't completely tattooed up like a biker or a rock star, but each arm had two old fashioned tattoos; one on each forearm and one on each bicep. Out of his janitors' clothing, he favored tight jeans and tight tee shirts that showed off his guns. He was one of those guys whose body cut up with definition, not from working out, but from eating less than fifteen hundred calories a day. He wasn't particularly strong, despite the bulging biceps and veiny arms. He worked with the janitorial staff at an office building on the Post Road and was constantly hopped up on bennies. After I knew him a bit better, he said to me in a hushed voice.

"Donnie, me, Paulie and Goat do a little side business selling prescription drugs whenever we can get a hold of them. You need anything, or you get some stuff, let me know. You're cool I know, Paulie told me, so this on the QT. I can also get you roids if you want'em."

I just listened and tried not to look in his direction. Diamond was so edgy and nervous, that looking at him made you edgy and nervous also.

I tried to avoid him as much as possible but he wouldn't leave me alone. After that first evening, I'd see Diamond quite a bit. He'd talk to me whenever he'd see me at the alleys, even though I tried to stay out of his way and tried as best I could to shoo him off. Then, he starting stopping by Goat's office and asking me to lunch. I always told him I was too busy, but he kept trying. If Goat was there when he stopped by, they'd go off together. I realized pretty quickly that Bramble was heavily tied in to most of Paulie and Goat's scams.

One night, I couldn't sleep and walked downstairs to the kitchen at two AM. Bramble was standing in the kitchen with Eddie Maguire and was handing him a bag. Neither one jumped as I walked into the room and Maguire calmly handed Diamond some cash. Paulie supposedly felt bad that Maguire was so strung out, but he didn't stop Bramble from being Maguire's supplier. That was the way it was in the thin line world; money always comes first.

After college, until it all collapsed, I always had money, more than I needed, so it was never special to me. It was there to spend and enjoy. However, struggling now, I started to think a bit like a thin liner. I made certain that Goat paid me in cash first thing Friday morning. If he tried to leave without paying me, I stopped him and made certain that I got my money. Occasionally, if I was running low, I let Paulie fill me up from one of his driveway city cans. I was always the guy who bought drinks for the house, now at the bowling alley I took whatever free stuff I could get. I hated to admit it but Paulie, Goat and Bramble were rubbing off on me.

Thirteen

Bramble had a girlfriend, Mary Ellen, a chunky blonde with a double chin who worked as a housemaid at the Marriott in West Haven. She lived with Diamond and her daughter, Eva, who was also a maid at the Marriott. Eva bowled with Paulie's crew and occasionally she went out with Goat.

Even when he was with Mary Ellen, Diamond hit on every girl that came near him and Mary Ellen just shrugged. I'm certain that he was on some sexual predator list, somewhere. For the single young girls at the alleys, some as young as sixteen, Diamond tried to act like their sugar daddy, although he had no real money and was just another thin liner looking for the next score. He'd buy them little gifts, pay for their drinks, and give them rides when they needed them. Sometimes he'd leave Mary Ellen by herself while he went off with someone else.

On top of the normal girls from the lanes, every working girl from Bridgeport to Milford knew Diamond, and he approached any unattached female that walked into the AMX Bowling Alley. Diamond led me to Holly.

I was sitting in the bowling alley bar and sipping a coke, my drink of choice since I sobered up. Bars are not the best place for recovering addicts but I was with Paulie and his crew so what else could I do. Since the rehab, and except for that one awful night when I almost drank, I was on my best behavior sticking with soda. We had already bowled and Paulie and Mary were dancing to the bar's juke box. Goat had gone home and Bramble came over to me. Behind him were two college-age kids; one a small, blonde girl with short hair, about twenty and the other a tall, skinny guy about my height and probably the same age as the girl. Bramble motioned to them and they walked forward and he introduced me. "Hey Donnie, I want you to meet these kids. I told them you're a good guy and a good friend of mine." The girl came toward me and held out her hand. "Hi Donnie, I'm Holly Meachem." She was no more than five two but with a hot young body, honey blonde hair and blue eyes that sparkled. She had the type of voice that made me in my younger days melt. She shook my hand formally like she was meeting a professor or someone else in authority. It seemed odd. "This is my boyfriend Matt," and she pointed to the guy behind her. He just nodded and said nothing. "We're students at UB and Diamond gets us some jobs occasionally," she told me. Then she looked over her shoulder to check that Diamond couldn't hear and she relaxed a bit and whispered, "he's a creep but he's nice to us."

"Donnie, you're good looking," she blurted out suddenly and her gaze seemed to be fixed onto my face. I was startled; she was cute but way too young for me, although even in my late fifties my brains were still located between my legs. "I bet you're nice to your kids," and she smiled.

I was flattered and surprised. "Holly, you're blowing up my ego. Most days, I'm invisible to any woman under thirty," and I laughed.

She shook her head to contradict me. "Donnie, you look good to me," and she seemed like she meant it.

Matt pulled her away and they walked out onto the dance floor. Bramble sat down next to me. "Pretty nice, eh Donnie?" Diamond said. "I think she likes you. I pointed you out and she asked to meet you. You can thank me later if you get anything." He looked over at her dancing. "Great ass," he said and snickered. "You don't see it right away but she and her boyfriend have an H-problem. I give them little jobs to get them cash for their dope. It might not show but they're pretty fucked up."

Hearing that about Holly was especially depressing, although anything is possible out here on the edge. I had just met the girl but there was a sweetness about her that didn't fit the profile of a junkie. She had something special that I couldn't quite wrap my fingers around. In the few words that she had spoken to me, and in the few moments that we had together, I had quickly, and perhaps foolishly, built a mental picture of her as a fun-loving college girl. Dope and working for Bramble were not part of the picture.

After Diamond told me about the dope problem, I watched her and her boyfriend dancing. They were the youngest dancers out there and made a nice couple. In my mind, she was appealing and a real honey but I made an effort to erase any thoughts about her in that direction. She was eight years or so younger than my daughter Gina, whom I hadn't seen at all in over four years. Gina had gotten married and in an act of reconciliation, she invited me; not to walk her down the aisle, she wouldn't have that, but just to be there. On the wedding day, I was all dressed but then I got drunk in my apartment and never showed up at the ceremony. My brother, Mikey, told me that I had a grandson, Gene, a big baby with a Celtic face. At his first birthday, Mike got me the picture I have on my dresser. I've been too ashamed to even try to see the boy and after all this time, and after missing the wedding, Gina wouldn't let me anyway. Right now, I do my best to push all those memories aside and just survive.

Fourteen

There was no reason to head home and Mary and Paulie were still dancing, so I sat by myself in the bar, sipped the coke and watched the dance floor. The music was pleasant so I stayed there and spaced out; mostly oblivious to the rest of the crowd. A half hour passed by and I got up to hit the men's room. Matt, Holly's skinny boyfriend caught me by the bathroom door. He was rail thin, wearing a short sleeve shirt that showed off beanstalk arms, but he was tall and looked at me eye to eye. "You want her, Cammond?" he asked, "a hundred bucks."

At first, nothing registered, and I had no idea what he was asking. He repeated it. "She likes you, so I'll make it cheaper than normal, a hundred bucks. Take her back to your place. I'll pick her up later. Diamond knows where Paulie lives. I can get there."

Then it all hit me, the stuff with the H problem, and Diamond getting them work. This sleazebag turned her out for the dope money and Diamond was acting as a second pimp. Like every other bad decision, I've made, I should have turned it down, but I glanced over and saw her looking at me. She was smiling as when we were talking and all that I saw were sweet, young, blue eyes and an alluring body. She was younger and better looking than I had been with in a very long time. I nodded yes at her and she started to walk over. "Give me the hundred now," Matt said.

"I'll pay her," I told him curtly, and then led Holly out to my car.

On the ride back to Stratford she chattered away, like the schoolgirl she was. I knew she was hooking and I knew about the dope but there seemed to be no hard edge to her. Holly was either one of the world's greatest actresses or where life had taken her hadn't yet impacted her personality. I couldn't decipher which it was.

"I'm a psych major," she told me during the ride. "I graduate next year, I hope, and I'm looking to go to graduate school." She looked over and I could see her studying my face. "Donnie, don't think bad of me. I liked the way you looked and you seemed sweet so I suggested it to Matt. We need the money. I don't do too many dates; this is just a part time thing."

There was an innocence about her that I liked immediately. Nothing about how she acted in private fit the lifestyle of a junkie hooker.

She was wearing tight jeans and a lacy shirt that showed off her magnificent young chest and while she studied my face, I had trouble keeping my eyes off of her. "You'll see the whole package soon enough," she laughed, "keep your eyes on the road."

Back in Stratford, I parked in Paulie's driveway and took her into the house. Having Holly beside me made the Sojak place seem even more tired, dingy and sad than usual, but she was still upbeat and talking away as I took her upstairs. I knew it was fake, and I knew I was paying her, but that didn't change the fact that it felt good having her by my side or the warm feeling as she held my hand. We could hear McGuire watching TV behind the closed door in his room as we walked by. "Is that Eddie Maguire in there?" She asked. "I know he lives here. I've seen him talking to Diamond."

"Yes," I told her. "You saw him with Bramble? I've hardly ever seen him leave the room."

"Yeah, I saw them talking at the alleys. I know Diamond gets him pills. I think he's gay. Diamond had a girl for him but he turned her down."

She said everything matter-of-factly; buying pills, Maguire gay, Diamond trying to set him up. Her manner and her sweet young voice were endearing and I was getting hooked.

Once inside my tiny room, she immediately started to unbutton her blouse. I didn't want it like that, just sex and nothing else; I wanted it to be something. I put my hand on her arm to stop her from getting undressed, then pulled her over to me and kissed her. I could feel her small body melting into my large frame. At first, she was surprised, but then kissed me back and I felt something special inside; perhaps a long forgotten young man's memory. Her mouth was soft and warm and her kisses seemed real. We stood kissing for quite a while and then, still dressed, I lay down with her on my bed. We then made love like lovers, slowly and passionately.

My bed in the Sojak house was small and uncomfortable, and she was petite, so I had to have her on top of me. When we finished, she rolled off of me and in the small space left of the bed, cuddled next to my side. She had her head in the crook of my neck and it felt right; like she belonged there. The comfort of the bed was no better with Holly next to me, yet for those few moments it felt wonderful and natural having her beside me.

She hugged me like it had all meant something, but I was embarrassed. She was so young. What was I thinking?

"It was really nice, Donnie," she told me in an almost whisper.

"You don't have to say that, Holly. I enjoyed it, though."

"No, I really mean it. You're a nice man." She kissed my neck.

We lay there together for a while and I could have made love to her a second time, but at my age I didn't want to risk not being able to, so I stood up and looked at her. Her lovely naked body was amazing, tight and alluring, and whether it was really that nice or just an older man's fantasy, who knows.

"Holly, you are beautiful," was all I could say to her.

She smiled that sweet schoolgirl smile and then said again, "Donnie, you are really a nice man. You don't fit with Diamond and the others."

I shrugged. "That's the way it is for me now, Holly."

She then stood up and dressed. I stared at her like a teenager with his first conquest. It was stupid. She was a hooker and I had had many women over the years, but I admired her like a young boy in love. She smiled at me the whole time she was dressing.

I wanted to do something to show her that it had been special. I handed her a hundred and fifty dollars and she looked at it and shook her head.

"No, Donnie, Matt said it was only a hundred," she said to me.

"It was special, Holly, keep the extra fifty. Don't give it to Matt."

She again shook her head, "You don't have to do that, Donnie," and held out fifty dollars for me to take back.

"I want to, Holly. Please take it."

I really couldn't afford the money, and certainly not the extra fifty. Part of me said take it back, the gesture was enough, but she put all the cash in her pocket and I was happy that she did.

Fifteen

We never made love or had sex again, but Holly became a part of my life. She and her boyfriend started to hang out with Paulie and his friends at the bowling alley, and then they started to come over to Paulie's house. From little snippets of the conversation that I heard, it was clear that Matt was becoming a part of Paulie and Goat's scam crew and Holly was not an uninvolved bystander. She was not the innocent girl that I had thought she was. Diamond helped her sleazy boyfriend pimp her out and she developed a clientele from some of the bowling lanes' regulars. There were several girls working AMX and she became the star, young and hot and the best looking there. It went beyond hooking, though. She and Matt stole what they could from her clients and she started giving Paulie and Goat stolen goods to fence for them or credit cards to use in a hurry. There were almost no complaints, though. Very few of the type of men who went into the bowling alley complained if a hooker scammed them. For them, it was better to be burned and keep it secret.

Holly was not innocent but she was complicated. She always tried to make some time, either at the lanes or at Paulie's house, to talk and flirt with me. I felt that she had the same type of young girl-daddy figure crush on me that Mary had. I have to say that having two young women, one quite beautiful, trying to hang out with me, blew up my ego. I didn't mind it at all.

When she was with me, Holly acted the part of a loving schoolgirl and she played that part to the hilt. With Paulie's crew, she would be part of all sorts of shitty thin line grifter plans and though I knew about them, I refused to believe them of her. They never matched the Holly that would wind up alone with me. In the bowling alley bar, while Diamond and Matt and the others planned out their foolish scams, she would sit and talk and talk to me, as if the others were nothing to her. She had dreams like every other twenty-year-old; graduate school, a career, a home, a husband. That she was living as a hustler and a thin liner never intruded on her fantasies. She held my hand and told me, her eyes fixed on mine, "Donnie, when I have my first kid, I want you to be the godfather. You know what's right and you're the only one who cares." I wanted to protect her, to get her off the thin line. I wanted her to be the sweet college student she pretended to be; the same sweet college student that she had become in my fantasies. I wavered back and forth. I knew it was stupid but I couldn't shake what I felt about her.

It happened six weeks after I first met her. She was arrested for buying drugs. I was sitting in Paulie's kitchen and he came in alone clearly agitated. Still, without much emotion he told me, "Donnie, Holly got busted for possession and buying. She's being held in Bridgeport." He filled in more details. "Matt, that stupid boyfriend of hers, he's a total asshole, sent her into a project near State

Street in Bridgeport to score some dope. Fucking kids are never careful and she got picked up by the Bridgeport PD. It was a fucking sting. These fucking kids are so stupid."

"How bad is it? She's going to need a lawyer," I answered.

Paulie shrugged his shoulders. "It's not so bad. Lucky for her, it was below the limit that's considered intent to sell; formal charge was just possession. It was heroin so it could be serious."

Even with all my years using oxy, except for the DUI, I never got involved with the court system. What could happen with selling or buying was foreign to me. "Just how serious, Paulie?" I cared about what would happen to Holly.

"Possession, they usually just give probation." Paulie answered, "Mary has two or three clicks for possession of coke, I don't remember exactly, but I know they treat crack and H tougher. You never know if some judge has a wild hair up his ass and wants to make an example of some college kid."

All this made me nervous. "Does she have a lawyer?"

Paulie nodded yes. "I got her the Greek's cousin, Panos. He handled Mary's cases."

I knew that Panos was incompetent. Angelos was better and of course connected to both the PD and the prosecutor's office, but he was disbarred and couldn't do anything official. Nor did he want to. He considered Holly to be part of Goat's crew and he was still angry over the charge card that Goat had never fully repaid.

I didn't want Holly doing time or spending any time at all at Bridgeport Correctional, which I was told was the absolute worst. A pretty white girl like her would be open meat for the tough black women that they had down there. My first instinct was to call my brother Mikey in Florida to see if he still knew anyone well enough to get a favor. But then I nixed that idea. Mikey would ask me what I was doing sticking my neck out for a twenty-year-old hustler/junkie and it was too tough for me to come clean on any of that. Still, Holly needed some help and more help than Paulie and his bunch could get her.

Panos got her out on bail, and she and Matt came over to Paulie's who gave the two of them the other empty bedroom. Matt left her there and it gave me the opportunity to talk to her alone. "Holly," I told her, "you have to get someone better than Panos. You could be facing real time. I hear judges are getting tougher and you don't want to get one that wants to make an example of a college student. What about your folks? You must have family that can help you."

"Fuck my family," she spit out, "they don't give a shit."

My first instincts were that she had an abusive redneck family but then she filled me in on her background. Up to that point, she had been evasive and secretive whenever anything about her past came up. As she talked, her demeanor changed and it looked like she was about to cry. "My father is a psychiatrist in Westport. He's a big-shot in the town and he's rich too."

"Then he can help you," I told her.

"I don't want their help; they don't give a shit."

She told me that she was his only child. "They adopted me. My real mother was a junkie and Dr. Meachem and

Charlotte adopted me. All they wanted was a little show thing; always had a nanny and they never ever paid any real attention to me."

Though it seemed to me that she had wound up in a nice situation, Holly had been nothing but trouble since starting high school; drugs and sex, and part of whatever bad crowd there was in a high-class town like Westport. Despite her sweetness to me, she was unapologetic about her past and hated the Meachems. She had several earlier arrests for possession and I had no idea how those would play out with the latest charge.

"I got in trouble and I got in trouble but he used his fucking money to clear it up," she told me without even a hint or remorse. "Most of my friends got put away or thrown out of school." Holly was different at different times, I knew that, but this was a hard and bitter Holly that told me all this. I listened but I wished I hadn't heard what I'd heard. It was clear that Dr. Meachem, her adopted father, had paid a fortune cleaning up Holly's problems and making the consequences disappear. She still despised him. "He's an asshole, Donnie. He just cares about his position in the community. He wanted a sweet pretty little child to show off to his friends. And Charlotte, my adopted mother, she's just the same. Does her nails, plays her tennis and wants me to be good." She started to laugh. "They think that Matt is good for me, helping me and all. They have no idea what he does."

She had to address the immediate problem and I had to have her realize it. "I don't care how you feel about your father, Holly," I told her, "you had better call him. Let him get a real lawyer here, before Panos gets you sent to

Niantic and you become a play thing for some big, black hooker up there."

Initially, she resisted my advice and did nothing, relying on Panos to do what he could. I kept pressing her. "Holly, Panos is a fucking moron and you have no idea how bad prison can be." Like Paulie, she believed that I had been in stir and until she did get her father to help, I was glad that she believed that. Eventually, she called her father, who hired David Axel, a top tier criminal attorney from Stamford. Axel painted for Holly and her parents the frightening picture of what Niantic Prison would be like for a small, wealthy blonde like Holly. They told him to do whatever he had to, either get her off or get her a light sentence.

The trial was in Bridgeport Superior Court and I went to the trial and sat in the back and watched. There were a whole bunch of drug cases on the docket and the courtroom was packed with junkies and other losers. Most of the lawyers were public defenders, equally divided between young kids just starting out and worn out old attorneys with either no skill like Panos, or nothing better to do. I told Holly not to acknowledge me but I wanted to make certain that Axel handled everything correctly. I shouldn't have worried. Axel wasn't connected to the local Bridgeport people but knew exactly how to play the system. He arranged to be the first case heard and he knew what to say. "Your honor, my client clearly has a drug problem, we admit that. She needs treatment, not prison. What she purchased was not with intent to sell."

The judge, Harold Bergman, was white haired, red-faced and listened to Axel with a look of exhaustion. He had heard every variation possible of a drug plea. He studied the papers Axel had given him looked at Holly and made his decision.

"Mr. Axel, I'm putting your client on two years' probation with the stipulation that she goes into drug rehab. The rehab will be monitored by this court and you have to report back to me once it is completed."

Axel nodded his head. This was what he had expected. "Thank you, your honor," was his only reply and Holly's case was done. The bailiff started to call the next case.

In the courtroom, I saw her father and mother. They were typical wealthy Westporters, too much money, coupled with an air of being above it all. Still, I couldn't help feeling sorry for them. Holly had raked them over the coals and her father had laid out a fortune to protect her from the worst consequences. About his daughter, Dr. Meachem was as thick as the thin liners and part of me wanted to shake him. "Look, Dr. Meachem, she needs tough love now. Let her feel the sting of what she's done." I said nothing, because I also wanted her protected from the worst. If Meachem's money could shield her, let it shield her. The mixture of love and pain that Dr. Meachem felt for his daughter sat openly on his face. Anyone who looked could see the anguish. When Bergman gave his decision, the Meachems sighed in relief. Axel turned and gave them a subdued thumbs up and they both smiled and hugged each other. Holly had once again dodged the worst, but she just looked impassive and nodded at the judge's decision.

As a psychiatrist, looking for the best possible treatment, her father shopped the various state rehabs.

Without any input from me, Holly wound up going to the same rehab, High Ridge Farm, that I had been to. I'm certain that he spoke to Elena McCann and she had sold him on their program. He was a parent looking for anything and Elena promised a chance at recovery for his daughter. Dr. Meachem gladly paid for the court mandated three weeks stay.

I knew that Holly going to the rehab was just scamming the poor father again, but I would have done the same. It was the rehab or jail time and what chance did she have at jail time. She was probably tough enough to survive but being with the other junkies and felons would only harden her further. I was aware that as small a chance as there was, the High Ridge program at least offered a glimmer of hope.

Dr. Meachem and his wife came to the Sojak house in his Mercedes to drive her to the facility in Kent. Matt went with them. From my second floor window, I watched them leave. The four of them appeared more like they were going on an outing or a car tour than taking a young girl to a rehab facility. Holly was bubbly and laughing as they went into the car and both her father's and mother's faces had a look of *maybe this time it will work.*

Sixteen

I visited Holly twice at the rehab and then suggested that she move in permanently and stay with Paulie in his sober house. What was I thinking? In the back of my mind, I thought that I could protect her there but I knew that I couldn't. Still, I wanted her close. After she left the rehab, she moved into Paulie's. Although it was against the state rules, Paulie let her boyfriend live there also.

Holly quickly went back to the lifestyle she had before, hustling. The Sojak house became her base of operations. Her father paid the rent and he and his wife were ecstatic at the prospect of her living in a place where someone would monitor her. They had no idea what a bad decision it was and there was no way I could tell them.

For Paulie, it was the perfect opportunity. She lived in the house and when Mary wasn't around, he did Holly for free, sort of a tax on Holly and Matt for living in his place. Mary, who could be jealous, turned a blind eye to it. Paulie pocketed the rent money anyway. Coming from Dr. Meachem, the cash was always on time. For a scammer like Paulie, it was an ideal situation.

Within a week or so, Holly also went back to using. There was no incentive for her to stop and Matt was still strung out. Bramble and Matt continued to turn her out at the bowling alley and she took her dates to a small motel in Milford. Mary told me that Matt had asked Paulie if Holly could use the house; he would pay Paulie something of course, but Paulie turned him down. It was too risky with the town of Stratford and there were people in the city who were looking for the opportunity to shut Paulie down. I wanted her to stop using and to stop hustling but she ignored what I said to her.

Once a week, Holly and Matt drove to Westport to visit her parents and to keep up the appearance of being straight. The two of them then began stealing little items from her father who had a bunch of different valuable collections; coins, stamps, art work, even old military uniforms. Paulie and Goat would deal them for her and then take a small cut for themselves. They had ties with all the fences on the Connecticut coast and there were never questions as to where the items came from. I tried talking to her.

"Holly, you can't keep stealing stuff. You're going to get caught and you're on probation. You know what I told you about Niatic. You'd be eaten alive there."

She listened and pretended to understand. "Donnie, I know you're right but it's for Matt. We'll be careful, I promise."

There was nothing further I could do but still my conscience ate at me. I never paid any attention to my own children, yet somehow, they had turned out all right. Both my boys eventually got out of college and they're working and my daughter is married with a child; it's killing me that I've never seen my grandson, but I guess that's the price I have to pay for all I did. As my dad might have said, "If you cover bad walls with paint, they look good for a while but the rot eventually comes to light." With those things in the back of my mind, I didn't want to just walk away from Holly, leave her to her own weaknesses but I did.

There isn't much honor among thin liners, only the next big score, and stealing from one another is no big deal. Paulie had a decent collection of tools in his garage and he never took any sort of inventory. Matt spotted the tools and realized that Paulie had no idea exactly which tools he had, so he and Holly pilfered a bunch of them. They weren't worth a fortune but it still amounted to a fair amount of cash. They sold what they stole to Dan Costa, a plumber in Milford, without realizing that he was an associate of Goat's. Costa then turned around and tried to sell the tools to Goat, who, when he looked at them, recognized them as Paulie's. Paulie laid out six hundred dollars to buy back his own tools. When he found out that Costa had bought them from Holly and Matt, he went apeshit.

"Those two fucking kids robbed from me," he ranted in Goat's office where he stopped off most afternoons to get coffee. "After all I done for her; took her in, got her a lawyer, help her out with stuff she's got to sell, and then she steals from me."

I just listened, there was nothing for me to add but Goat had the thin liner perspective. "Paulie, you're fucking her for nothing. What are you complaining about? Besides you got the tools back and you don't use them anyway."

"It's the principle, Goat. She robbed me," Paulie said, oblivious to the fact that any loyalty principle was meaningless in his world. "I'm throwing her and that fucking greasy boyfriend out the door; out on their asses where Diamond found them."

He confronted Matt. With me, probably out of fear, Paulie never played the tough guy, but with Matt, who had only about a hundred thirty pounds on his scrawny six-two frame, Paulie acted like Mike Tyson or Sonny Corleone. "You stole my fucking tools, you ungrateful greasy bastard. You and Holly are out of here."

Matt surprised me. He shook his head, looked Paulie right in the eye and stayed calm. "Yeah Paulie, we took the tools. They were just sitting in the garage and we were going to pay you back anyway. We appreciate everything you've done for us."

"Pay me back, yeah right. You're out the door," Paulie told him, "unless you get me the cash and soon." To a scammer like Paulie, despite what he said about principle, all that mattered was the money. "It cost me six bills, you prick, to get my tools back. I want that money and a fine for taking them – eight hundred bucks."

Matt kept his composure, shook his head and walked away; a day or so later, he handed Paulie eight crisp one hundred-dollar bills. Holly told me that she had asked her father for it. Told him it was for school. The eight hundred dollars that Matt gave Paulie smoothed conditions over, eased any anger, and things went back to normal.

Seventeen

A few days after the stolen tools, Holly and Matt came to Paulie with plans for a big score. They needed Paulie and Goat to convert their plan into cash.

Dr. Meachem had among his collections, valuable stamps. According to Holly, her father had spent years putting his stamp collection together and each of his albums was worth a fortune. Now, she told Paulie, the old man hardly ever looked at his albums. He kept them in a special room in his house, along with his coins and a military uniform collection; a museum room to show visitors. If they took one or two, her father wouldn't notice that they were missing. If, on the odd chance that he did, he'd probably suspect Holly, but he wouldn't say anything; at least, she didn't think he would. She told Paulie that she would give him one of the albums but he'd have to use his connections to sell the stamps. Paulie and Goat agreed. This was the type of scam that was right up their alley; stolen stamps that they didn't steal, just had to unload.

Holly swiped an album and gave it to Paulie, who had it appraised by a dealer he knew in New Haven. The dealer put the value of that book by itself at over fifty-five thousand. The local scumbags that Paulie and Goat regularly dealt with didn't have that kind of cash, or wouldn't handle something that big.

Louie Cataro was an older, community respected businessman who lived in West Haven. He owned an antiques shop, but made most of his money as a fence for the local thieves. Lou was tight with Paulie and Goat, and Paulie invited him to the house. By now, although I hadn't taken part in any scam, Paulie trusted me and I sat in the kitchen with them as Paulie laid out his plan to Cataro. "Louie, it's a piece of cake. This doctor's never going to miss the stamps. I'm guaranteed that. Gianozza, the dealer up in New Haven puts them at over fifty-five large. All you got to do is deal them for me. No risk – all cash."

Cataro listened and shook his head. "No way Paulie I would touch that. Never anything guaranteed. This doctor turns around and brings in the cops and we're fucked. It's too big. I told you Paulie, never do anything too big. Stay small, keep the cash and it keeps the law away. As soon as you push too far, that's when trouble starts."

Every other local fence also brushed them off, but Paulie and Goat wouldn't let go. The stamp collection made their eyes huge and made their mouths water. It was to be the biggest scam of their lives and it clouded their judgment, what little judgment they had. Through Panos, Angelos the Greek's cousin, Paulie found a dealer in New York City who would assess the album, deal with it and ask no big questions. The problem was that this dealer knew Paulie and Goat by reputation as small timers with limited smarts. He didn't trust them a bit. They needed a new go-between, so they approached me.

"Look, Donnie," Paulie started, "you don't have to do anything. Take the stamp book to New York and show it to this guy. He'll give you a price and I'm trusting that you can negotiate something good. I got a value here for over sixty G's but I'll go down as low as forty buying price if that's the best you can do. Look, you get me at least forty, and I'll cut you in for two grand."

The two thousand didn't mean much to me. Sure, I needed the money, I was still just barely scraping by working for Goat, but I didn't want to get involved with anything crooked. My head kept telling me "Stay on the right side of the line. Don't go there; be smart." What meant something to me was not being a part of their thin line deals. I also didn't like the fact that Holly had stolen it. I kept hoping that she'd somehow see the light.

After he asked me, I shook my head and hesitated. For me, if I did this for them, I was finally crossing that line and there was no going back. My father, my mother, Father Brendan and all that church sat there in my conscience, no matter how far out on the rim I found myself. It was one thing hanging out with all these thin liners and ignoring what they did, but it was a step over the line if I got involved. As soon as I pocketed any money, I was just one of them; no more, no less. I didn't want that, I wanted to keep my private superiority; but I did need the money and it was an easy task. Hanging out with them for all those months had rubbed off on me.

Paulie assumed that my hesitation was about the money. "Donnie, listen, we're trusting you with something important here. You do it, I'll up your piece to twenty-five hundred. Come on, Donnie, you'll be doing us a big solid."

I tried to rationalize, find reasons for doing this. Maybe I could use the money to help Holly; help her get away from the life. I tossed it back and forth in my mind and then convinced myself, against my conscience, to take the wrong turn. "All right Paulie, you tell me where I have to go and what exactly I have to do."

"It's easy, Donnie. You go into New York. You go to the dealer. He'll know who you are and what it's all about. All you do is negotiate a price and bring the cash back. Then you pocket a cool two and half thou."

Eighteen

Even after telling Paulie that I would do it, I kept turning the decision over in my mind. Did I really want to be a part of their scam? If I did this, it was only the beginning. I knew it. I spoke to Holly when we were alone. She was happy that I was doing this for her.

"Donnie, thank you so much. I'm glad you're going into the dealer. I'm certain that Paulie or Goat or even Matt would screw this up. You're classy, you can handle it."

I shook my head. "Holly, I told Paulie I would do it, but we really shouldn't. Why don't you put it back with your dad's other stuff before everything blows up? There's a lot of money involved here. When he notices that it's missing, he's not going to just sit by. He's going to know that you took it."

Holly got angry and it was first time that I saw her real hardened persona. "Fuck my father, Donnie. He has all the fucking money he needs. I'm taking these."

Why she hated her parents so much was never clear and I didn't want to go there. I wanted the sweet Holly and this hardened Holly frightened me. "Holly, I said I would do it, and I'll do it for you."

Eventually the lure of the money, as small as it was for me, and the fact that I convinced myself that I was doing it for Holly won out.

On the following Tuesday, I got dressed up for the trip into Manhattan. I put on my one business suit that I had kept from my days in the computer business. That was the image I wanted to project to the dealer in New York; well-established businessman. It was also how I wanted to think of myself. I would negotiate and sell the stamp collection but it was all legit, just a business deal. I wanted to feel and act like I had never rolled downhill, never gotten to the edge. That's how I wanted it to come off.

With my suit and tie on, I had the feeling I was ready for battle. My father always admired a newly painted room if it was done well and I felt like I put on a new coat of paint. I took a quick look at myself in the small mirror in my room, straightened my collar, and then went down to the Sojak house kitchen. Paulie and Goat were waiting for me.

Paulie told me to sit down and the two of them then began to give me instructions. The two of them were nervous; this was a huge scam and really out of their league. Their words were flying at me and most of what they said made no sense. I assumed that one of them would take the trip to New York with me, but it was clear that they were leaving me on my own and relying on me to pull off the whole deal.

"Look, Donnie, I know you can handle it," Paulie said to me. "But you have to remember this guy Antoine is classy and the stamps, well, you don't where we got them but they're all legit. You understand that, Donnie?" Goat sat behind him like a hungry dog and nodded at each thing he said.

I nodded that I knew what was necessary and there was nothing to worry about but they went through the whole procedure several times.

"You get us at least forty-five thou. I'm counting on you, Donnie. It has to be cash; you have to tell him that. No bank checks or anything. Antoine knows all this but he still might try to give you a check." Paulie was adamant about getting cash.

I held out my hands to calm Paulie and Goat down and told them for the third or fourth time, "Look, Paulie, I know what I have to do. I can handle this."

I stuffed Antoine's address and phone number into my pocket and started to walk to the door. "I have to catch the 10:30 train. Paulie, don't worry, I'll take care of everything."

Goat, who up to this point had only listened, now cut in. "Listen, Donnie, don't you go thinking you're going to rob us. We'll give you your cut." There was no part of Goat's world that he trusted, least of all me. Why he wasn't coming with me, I had no idea, but to him the possibility that I would rip them off was very real. He couldn't picture someone who wouldn't bite on a sixty-thousand-dollar apple.

"Goat," I shook my head, "I just want my cut. You can trust me. What I want is that you guys treat Holly fairly."

"Yeah sure, Donnie, we'll take care of her." They both said it but it was a half-hearted affirmation.

Nineteen

I took the train to Manhattan, got off at Grand Central and then walked to a building on Third Avenue and Forty-Ninth. I stood on the street in front of the building and then dialed the number on Antoine's card from my cell. A receptionist told me to come on up and I took an elevator to a second-floor office; Antoine Delacorte Enterprises. There was no indication on the door exactly what the enterprises were. I gave my name to the receptionist, a young, good-looking, Hispanic woman in a tight blouse wearing dark glasses and she told me to have a seat. Less than five minutes later, a very well-dressed, slender bald man, Antoine, greeted me and ushered me into his office. He was fastidious looking with a lavender shirt and tie and a matching vest with no suit jacket. Once inside, he had me sit on a couch. He never offered me a handshake and he made it clear by his manner that there was to be no chit chat. Very formally, he said to me, "Mr. Cammond, I've already spoken to Mr. Sojak, Let me see the stamps and we'll take it from there."

I had the stamp album wrapped in a Lord and Taylor bag and I handed it to him. He took it to his desk. "This will take a while, Mr. Cammond. There are magazines, if you'd like to read. Would you like some coffee?" I waved off the coffee offer and sat back on the couch while he started to pore over the stamps. He had taken out some other material as well as a magnifying glass. He asked me nothing.

He examined the stamps, constantly referring to some other book that I assumed had buying prices, and worked for over an hour at his desk. I read through an old New Yorker and part of the Times. He then walked back to me.

"It seems to be in order, Mr. Cammond. I'll give him forty-five thousand for this collection." He held out an envelope. "It's all there. You can count it if you like."

Paulie had told me to negotiate and that the appraiser in New Haven had put the value at close to sixty thousand. On the other hand, he had told me to accept forty. I was never a haggler. I had been a good software salesman, but in the software business, the prices were cut and dried. Everyone knew what everything was worth. Back then, when I worked in the industry, I did make deals to get sales, but prices were prices. I wasn't going to haggle here. I took the envelope and counted the cash. Forty-five thousand in hundreds and I didn't have to fight over cash versus a check. After counting, I stood up. "Well, as you said Mr. Delacorte, it seems to be in order."

I held out my hand to shake his. Antoine shook my hand weakly and I left. In the hallway, before taking the elevator down, I pulled out my twenty-five hundred and slipped it in my suit pocket, away from the cash envelope. Better to take my cut-up front. I was thinking like a thin liner.

I slept on the train ride back. The tension had taken a lot out of me. At the Sojak house, I handed the envelope to Paulie. Goat sat behind him like a hungry dog and stared at the cash.

"He offered me thirty but I juiced it up to forty-five," I lied to them. I then told them, "I already took my cut."

The two of them were ecstatic over the deal and for once, one of their scams seemed to have worked out.

Dr. Meachem realized that one of his albums was missing and suspected Holly immediately. He went to the Westport police and an investigator came to Stratford, who then questioned Paulie about Holly. He told Paulie that there was a theft at the Meachem house and he was covering all possibilities. The investigator intimated that he had known Holly and all her drug trouble throughout the years and she was his number one suspect. Paulie managed to finesse the investigator and they seemed to be in the clear. He and Goat told Holly that they had better forget about any more of the stamps.

Yet, their scam seemed to have gone over with only that minor glitch and Paulie, Goat, Mary, Holly and Matt went for a celebration dinner at Palazzo, an Italian restaurant in West Haven. They invited me, but I declined. I had crossed the line and that tore at me. I looked in the mirror in my tiny room and asked, "Am I really the same as Diamond Bramble?"

I tried to maintain my attitude of looking down at all of them but it just wasn't inside me anymore. Helping with the stamp album scam had cut me down quite a few pegs. I put the cash in my room but after stashing it, I refused to look at it. I tried to avoid Paulie's crew and on their bowling nights, I stayed at home and read.

Paulie and his bunch had moved on to some new scam but Holly seemed as sweet as ever. One evening, Paulie, Goat and the rest were out somewhere and Holly was still in the house. I sat in the kitchen, reading. Holly walked out from her bedroom and took a glass of milk from the fridge. She had on sweat pants and an oversized sweat shirt and she looked as cute as ever. I sat quietly next to Paulie's clocks at the kitchen table and she asked me, "What's been the matter, Donnie, it seems like something's wrong? You're never with us anymore?"

"Nothing, Holly," I told her, "I'm just tired of living like this."

She sat down on my lap and slipped her head on my shoulder. "Let's run away, Donnie. You could take care of me." She snuggled softly against me and I couldn't help smiling.

"That would be really sweet, Holly, but you know it'll never happen."

She said nothing but sat softly on my lap for what seemed like forever. She then got up and walked into the bedroom and I went back to my newspaper.

Twenty

It was two weeks later, in the morning, and I sat alone in Paulie's small dining room. I pushed his clocks to one side of the table, and I was reading the newspaper and half-heartedly listening to the news on the small black and white TV that Paulie kept on a side table. Mary and Holly were still asleep and I assumed that Eddie Maguire was as usual in his room. Matt suddenly burst through the back door and barged into the kitchen. He had been gone for the past two days and he looked a mess. He nodded in my direction, without speaking, and then walked into Holly's bedroom. "Holy shit," he suddenly shrieked and then he started yelling, "get up, Holly, please get up."

I ran into the bedroom and Holly was lying motionless on the bed in just a bra and panties. There was a used needle on the nightstand. She was normally fair-skinned but lying there, she looked as white as a piece of crumpled paper. There was a sudden, sharp pain in my gut as if I'd been kicked and I knew it was the worst. I walked over and first learned over to her face, trying to feel a breath and then gently touched her neck looking for a pulse. Matt was shaking and crying. "You'd better call nine-one-one," he said between gasps of air.

I was shaking also, but I tried my best to stay calm. "Forget nine-one-one, she's dead already. Better just call the police."

The commotion had woken Mary who usually slept soundly and she wandered in wearing a loose nightgown with her ample bosom bouncing around. "What's going on?" she asked and then saw Holly's lifeless body. "Oh my God, is she dead?"

I nodded yes and Mary started to cry hysterically. I walked over and held her shoulders. Matt was dialing his cell. I assumed he was calling the police but he actually had dialed Paulie. "Donnie," he said and he handed me the phone, "it's Paulie. He wants to talk to you." I took the phone and Paulie started talking. "Donnie, you didn't touch her, did you?" I told him no and he continued. "Well, don't do nothing till I get home. I gotta figure out what to do."

Within ten minutes, Paulie walked in with Goat. Mary and Matt were still crying but had drifted out of the bedroom. I sat on a chair just staring at Holly. Paulie and Goat walked over to the body and felt for a pulse like I had done. Paulie spoke to both Goat and me. "She's definitely fucking dead. We have to move her out of here."

"Paulie, you have to call the police. You can't move her." I told him. Paulie shook his head "We've got to get her out of here. The town's out to get me and I'm not losing my license for this place because of a fucking junkie whore."

"Hey, Paulie," Goat started, "just go slow. We move her, you're inviting more trouble. I think moving a dead body is some sort of felony. Think about it. You thought she was following the rules. You can't control every minute."

Paulie was silent and then said, "I have to think. Donnie, let me talk to Goat. You get out of here."

The sharp pain in my gut got worse. It was a pain I had felt before. It was there when each of my parents had died but this was even stronger. It felt like I had been shot. I wanted to weep like Mary, to just break down and sob. In reality, Holly was nothing to me, but in her I found something that I cared about. I pitied her poor father who had invested all that effort for nothing and would now be alone in his grief. I sat down in a chair in the kitchen and pictured my whole life as it had rolled downhill. Holly had died but it was me that I felt sorry for. I saw that long thin line stretched out in front of me but now that line had become a canyon with Holly waving from across the other side.

Paulie and Goat walked out of the bedroom. "Listen, Matt, you get the fuck out of here. You saw nothing and know nothing. Get in your car and leave now. I'll take care of this." He turned next, to me, "Donnie, I'm calling the police but you take Mary out of here, can't have her here hysterical. I'll handle it and you know nothing either." I was still shaky but Paulie and Goat seemed calm. "Mary, go get dressed," Paulie told her, "Donny will take you to your mother's. You two just keep your mouths shut."

I took Mary to her parents' house on the other side of Stratford, then had a cup of coffee at a deli on the Post Road and then went back to the Sojak house. There was a coroner's truck and a bunch of police cars in the driveway. I walked in anyway. Paulie was standing in the kitchen being questioned by a cop. The cop turned to me. "Who are you?" he asked.

"Don Cammond, I live here. What's going on, Paulie?" I was playing the know nothing game.

"Holly OD'ed," Paulie told me.

"Oh shit," I said. "Poor girl couldn't keep it together."

"You an addict also?" the cop asked.

"Recovering. I've been clean almost four years."

"You know this Holly? You know she was using?"

"Of course I knew her. We lived together but I don't watch the other tenants. I follow the rules and stay to myself."

Maguire then came out his room in his underwear to use the bathroom. The cop looked at him and called him over. "Who are you?"

"Eddie Maguire. I'm a tenant. What's going on?"

The cop shook his head, almost in disbelief. "A girl died here. Where the hell were you all this time?"

"I was sleeping. I came in late last night. Who died?"

I thought to myself, "Oh shit, I hope they don't search Maguire's room. He had to have a stash of pills in there and they would look really bad for Paulie."

The cop just waved him away and Maguire left.

The cop turned back to Paulie. "Sojak, don't rent out the room until we say it's okay. We might consider it a crime scene."

"What kind of crime scene?" Paulie asked a bit annoyed. "She OD'ed. I can't watch her all the time."

"Just don't rent it until we say it's okay." The cop walked into the bedroom. In another twenty minutes, they had taken Holly's body away and the cops had left.

Twenty-One

Paulie claimed someone in the city government was out to get him, close him down but he bit the bullet on Holly's death. The police department called back a few days later and told him that there was no further investigation and he was free to rent the room.

Dr. Meachem held a small funeral in a Methodist Church in Westport. He and his wife were crushed. I went with Paulie, Goat and Mary to the service and then went out to the cemetery. Matt stood with the family like he belonged there. I wanted to wring his skinny neck. We walked in line after the service to give our condolences to the Meachems. "I tried my best sir, I'm sorry. I couldn't watch her all the time," Paulie told the doctor. He actually sounded sincere. The doctor was in shock but still cold to Paulie. He must have hoped that the sober house would keep her in line.

Paulie and the crew were appropriately somber at the funeral, but back in Stratford, they just returned to life as usual. Thin-liners never spend too much time pondering what they've done or what has happened. The next easy buck has to be found; the next scam planned out. People die, but the thin line life just goes on, and I hardly heard

Paulie or Goat mention Holly. Even Mary seemed to ignore what had happened.

I was crushed; much more that I would have expected. I didn't know what I was going to do, but I had to do something. I had crossed the thin line but maybe there was time to get back onto the right side of the highway.

A few days after the funeral, Paulie and Mary were at work and the house was empty. I called Goat and told him that I was sick. My head was unclear and I sat in the stuffy kitchen, unable to think. I drifted off to sleep but the church bells on the corner rang and I woke with a start. I walked over to the stove to make myself a coffee.

I hadn't heard my father's voice in years, he died over twenty years ago, but suddenly as clear as a bell, I heard it, with just the hint of the burr.

"Donny boy, you're not one of them, you're no thin-liner. Get yourself away."

It jarred and shocked me, hearing the voice. At first, I thought it was Maguire but then I heard it again with its reprimanding but commanding tone, "Donny boy, don't dawdle. Get away now."

I sat up straight and listened for more but nothing came. He had told me what he wanted to tell me. In death, as in his life, he was classic Scottish; terse and never said more than he had to. I had no plans, but I went up to my room and packed up what little I had. I carried them downstairs and then put them into my car. I took out the envelope with my twenty-five hundred cash and looked in at the money. It was dirty money and my inclination was to leave it behind, throw the bills on the kitchen table and let Paulie have them. I needed the cash, though, whatever I did, so I stuffed the bills into my pocket and went out to the car. I sat for a few moments on the front seat then took a long last look at the Sojak house and drove off.

At the filling station, just before the I-95 entrance, I filled my car with gas and then got on the interstate heading south and started to drive. I passed Bridgeport and then Stamford with no clear idea of where I was going to or what I was going to do.

I continued on through New York State and then went over the GW onto the Jersey Turnpike towards Washington. I sang to the songs on the radio to prevent myself from thinking. Finally, at a rest stop on the turnpike, somewhere in New Jersey, well past my old house, I called my brother Mikey, down in Ocala.

"Put me up for a while?" I asked.